THE BODY IN

Frenchie circled back, darting pas

dog. At least I'd be racking up steps o

"Come on, come here." I patted my leg.

She headed back toward the archery targets and I followed. Stopping behind one, she barked again. I hurried forward, thinking I could grab ahold of the leash and as I did, I tripped over something and fell to the ground, skidding across the grass. There went my pristine new exercise pants.

What on earth had I stumbled over?

Stunned by the impact, I slowly opened my eyes.

Sightless violet eyes stared back at me; perfectly platinum hair was matted with blood. She must have hit her head when she fell. But I didn't think it was the head wound that had killed Colette.

I was pretty sure it was the arrow sticking out of her chest…

Books by Mary Lee Ashford

GAME OF SCONES

RISKY BISCUITS

QUICHE OF DEATH

Published by Kensington Publishing Corporation

Quiche of Death

Mary Lee Ashford

LYRICAL UNDERGROUND
Kensington Publishing Corp.
www.kensingtonbooks.com

To the extent that the image or images on the cover of this book depict a person or persons, such person or persons are merely models, and are not intended to portray any character or characters featured in the book.

This book is a work of fiction. Names, characters, places, and incidents either are products of the author's imagination or are used fictitiously. Any resemblance to actual events or locales or persons living or dead is entirely coincidental.

LYRICAL UNDERGROUND BOOKS are published by

Kensington Publishing Corp.
119 West 40th Street
New York, NY 10018

All Kensington titles, imprints, and distributed lines are available at special quantity discounts for bulk purchases for sales promotion, premiums, fund-raising, educational, or institutional use.

Special book excerpts or customized printings can also be created to fit specific needs. For details, write or phone the office of the Kensington Sales Manager: Kensington Publishing Corp., 119 West 40th Street, New York, NY 10018. Attn. Sales Department. Phone: 1-800-221-2647.

First Electronic Edition: July 2020
ISBN-13: 978-1-5161-0508-3 (ebook)
ISBN-10: 1-5161-0508-7 (ebook)

First Print Edition: July 2020
ISBN-13: 978-1-5161-0509-0
ISBN-10: 1-5161-0509-5

Printed in the United States of America

Chapter One

"Quiche me, you fool."

The demand was followed by hoots of laughter as the sister—Jezzie, I think her name was—leaned into her spouse for a smooch. He hesitated but obliged.

I smiled at the boisterous group who clearly shared some inside joke about quiche and kissing. The warmth of the table and the sibling love melted my heart like butter on a biscuit. Taking a sip of water, I glanced over at Dixie, who sat across from me at the huge oak table.

She rolled her eyes.

"What?" I mouthed.

Dixie shrugged. Jezzie had perhaps a teensy bit too much wine, but still: When did my best friend and business partner get so darn stuffy? Maybe it was the inside-joke part that she found off-putting.

But we did know quiche was the family's stock-in-trade, so it wasn't that much of a stretch to figure out the expression had something to do with the Arbor family's food business. After all, that was why we were here.

I'm Sugar Calloway, the eye-roller is Dixie Spicer, and we own Sugar and Spice Cookbooks. Usually we do fundraising groups, nonprofits, schools, churches, and the like. But we'd worked with Gwendolyn Arbor, who was married to the younger brother of the clan, on a cookbook featuring Iowa's wonderful bed-and-breakfasts and their specialty recipes.

The project had been fun. And challenging. And fun. I guess, overall it had gone well, and when Gwen had contacted us about her in-laws wanting to put together a book of family recipes, we'd agreed.

Plans for getting everyone together for a weeklong visit for the matriarch of the family's birthday had included inviting us for the weekend as an efficient way to discuss which recipes should be featured. We'd arrived just before dinner.

Lucky us.

The food was mind-blowing. The family's famous quiche Lorraine, served with oven-roasted vegetables, fresh strawberry walnut spinach salad, and warm French bread.

I glanced around the table, hoping no one had noticed Dixie's eye roll.

There was Jezzie, the kisser, and her husband, Tom, a serious-looking, nondescript man. Jezzie was all polish and pizzazz. Dark hair like her siblings, but frosted with strategically placed silver highlights, a bright red jacket with apple-red lipstick to match. She was a fancy gourmet dish. And Tom? Well, if we follow the foodie comparison, he was a tuna casserole.

Beside them were Gwendolyn and her hubs, Jonathan. A former stockbroker, he'd left that life to move back to the area. According to Gwen, he'd developed an interest in historic renovations. Like I said, Gwen was the connection that had brought us into this project. She ran the Arbor House Bed-and-Breakfast and always looked to me like she could be a model for the mature professional women you see in magazine ads. Short silver curls, tall, slim, quietly elegant. A dove gray scarf wrapped around her shoulders. And Jonathan Arbor was the perfect foil. Distinguished looking, dark hair with a touch of gray at the temples.

Maybe it was my former life at a big-time food magazine that made me tend to see everyone in terms of food or advertisements.

Rounding out the group were Joe, Jr. who everyone called J.J., the oldest of the Arbor siblings, and his wife, Lucinda, who was chatting with Dixie in a low voice. Gwen had mentioned Lucinda was into genealogy and I hoped to talk with her sometime over the weekend about how to get started.

At the end of the heavy oak table, taking it all in, was Marta, the birthday gal and queen mum of the family. Her lined face was difficult to read, but her dark eyes didn't miss a thing. She took small bites and sipped her tea, but her eyes darted from one conversation to another.

Beside her were two empty chairs. There were place settings, so it seemed more people were expected. I didn't ask. You know, sometimes people have that tradition where they leave an empty chair for their dearly departed. I knew the patriarch of the family, Joseph Arbor, had departed a while ago and that the two oldest siblings ran Arbor Family Foods, the company he'd started. Maybe they left an empty chair at the table for him.

The food had been served family-style, so plates were being passed around. I'd just accepted an overflowing basket of French bread from Tom when I heard the door open and in blew a couple that completely changed the energy in the room.

"Theo!" Marta's face was no longer unreadable. The pure joy swept years from her and her pale cheeks bloomed with color.

The guy was handsome and shared the dark hair and coloring of the Arbor siblings, so my guess was that he was a family member and a favorite one, if Marta's reaction was any indication.

"Grand-mère." He knelt down and brushed a kiss on her cheek. Turning back to the girl he'd left standing in the doorway, he motioned for her to join him.

She was slender and petite; her shiny platinum hair a striking contrast to his dark coloring.

"My fiancée, Colette," he continued, turning to look at the rest of the group.

"Hello." She smiled, flipping a lock of blond hair and adjusting the toy poodle she held so she could give a wave. "Awesome to meet you."

Her bright pink jacket perfectly matched the pup's pink bow. I shifted my gaze from girl and poodle back to the table in time to catch a look on Jezzie's face that led me to believe she didn't think it was so awesome. Her son, perhaps? Overprotective mother? Maybe.

"And this is Frenchie." She lifted the dog and waved one of the tiny paws in greeting. Though how she could do it with the size of the rock on her ring finger I don't know. Don't get me wrong, I'm a fan of diamonds as much as the next girl but—wow.

"Nice to meet you. Hello." There were nods, waves, and a murmur of greetings.

I glanced back in Marta's direction, curious as to what she thought of the new soon-to-be-family member. She sat quietly, but I recognized the one-raised-eyebrow look. I'd seen it enough from my own mother and it usually meant, "We'll see about that." The jury was clearly out on whether Ms. Colette and pup were what the grand dame had in mind for Theo.

As I turned back to say something to Dixie, Gwen commented on Colette's ring. Lifting her hand to show it to advantage in the light of the chandelier, Colette put Frenchie down right on the big table amid the dishes.

The poodle, sensing a feast and that she had limited time, dove for the nearest plate. She snapped up a piece of quiche that had been left in the serving dish, gobbled up a nearby piece of asparagus, and then headed for the tray of chocolate mousse that Hilda, the woman who'd been serving, had just placed on the table in readiness for dessert.

Frenchie obviously thought dessert was a great idea and dove right in, burying her snout in the closest of the dishes, her wagging tail knocking over crystal water glasses in her excitement.

Colette lunged for the dog, upending even more glasses of water and wine, as the pooch—now covered in food—attempted to wriggle away.

"Chocolate can be deadly to dogs!" Colette scolded, as if the family had attempted to poison the poodle.

"So can walking around on the dinner table," Jezzie said under her breath, but apparently loud enough that Colette could hear.

"She's just an innocent dog," Colette gasped. "I can't believe you'd want to hurt her."

"Of course, she wouldn't." Theo scooped up Frenchie and handed her to Colette. By this time the poor pup had started to gag, whether from the excitement or the chocolate mousse I wasn't sure.

"Let's just take her outside for the moment." Gwendolyn stepped forward and turned Colette and the dog toward the door.

Hilda, the server, came back through the door with another tray of mousse, but stopped short when she took in the chaos.

"Would you bring some towels?" Gwendolyn asked over her shoulder. "And a mop."

Hilda nodded and exited. Jonathan, who'd been across from me, stood and began gathering the plates and knocked-over glasses.

"Shall we just clear this and we'll have our dessert and coffee in the living room?"

In a short time, Gwen was back. "I think the dog will be okay. She only ingested a tiny bit and pretty much none of it stayed down."

We all helped gather dishes and carry them to the kitchen. Then everyone made their way to the living room, but no one was much in the mood for relaxing with dessert and coffee.

Theo and Colette were off in a corner, whispering, and though the rest of the clan tried to make conversation, it was peppered with awkward silences.

After a little while, Dixie and I excused ourselves, begging off dessert after such a filling dinner. If this was a preview of the days to come, we were in store for one heck of a week.

* * * *

Because the B and B was full with all of the family staying, Dixie and I were sharing a large room on the third floor for the weekend. We'd dropped our luggage off when we'd arrived, but hadn't really had time to unpack.

The polished hardwood floor complemented the light peach tone of the walls, the matching duvets on the two double beds were a deep cranberry, and the crisp white pillowcases and luxurious linens made you want to crawl in bed immediately.

"I can see why the bed-and-breakfast does so well."

"What?" Dixie stuck her head out from the en suite bathroom, her mouth full of toothpaste.

"I said, I can see why Arbor House does so well," I repeated. "This is gorgeous."

"It is." She walked out, wiping her face with a peach-colored towel.

"What did you think of the family?" I asked.

"Too soon to say, but they seem nice enough." She took the towel back to the bathroom.

"They're all striking." I pictured each of them around the table.

"What do you mean, *striking*?" Dixie asked.

"You know, the dark hair—"

"You have dark hair," she interrupted. "Beautiful straight dark hair." She flipped one of her own red curls with a hand. "Trade you."

"Gladly. I have boring dark hair and gray eyes," I pointed out. "The Arbor family's jet-black hair and deep brown eyes are striking."

"Your dark hair and gray eyes, along with your porcelain skin, makes you more striking," she insisted.

"But—" I began.

"All right." Dixie rolled her eyes. "You win. They are *striking*."

"By the way, what was with the eye-rolling at dinner?" I asked.

"What are you talking about?" She gave me a quizzical look.

"During dinner when Jezzie was all kissy-face with Mr. Boring."

"Mr. Boring?" Dixie gave me a strange look. "Oh, you mean when they were misquoting Theda Bara?"

"Huh?"

"The quote is actually, 'Kiss me, my fool' and gets misquoted a lot." She pulled back the covers on the closest bed and plumped the pillows. "It's from an old silent movie about a woman who seduces men, takes their money, and then they kill themselves."

"Nice." I picked up one of my pillows and threw it at her. "Too much late-night movie channel for you. We need to get you out of the house more."

"I'm out of the house now," she said over her shoulder.

"So you are," I agreed. "It's a start."

"I can't think of the last time I slept anywhere other than my own bed. Let alone shared a room with someone." She patted the pillows in place. "I hope I don't snore."

"Won't bother me." I hunted for my small bag of toiletries to take my turn in the bathroom. I didn't see it and I was sure I'd packed it. I hoped I packed it.

"What are you looking for?" Dixie asked.

"I can't find my cosmetics bag." I pulled everything out of my suitcase for the third time. "Trust me, no one wants to be subjected to a weekend of me with no makeup."

"Is there anything in there you have to have right now?" Dixie continued arranging pillows and bedding. "Can't it wait until morning? I'll lend you anything you need."

"I put the charger for my activity tracker in there, and it will be dead tomorrow if I don't plug it in." Checking again around the area where we'd stacked our bags, I still didn't see it.

"Oh, no." Dixie rolled her eyes and this time I was the target. "You mean you might take some steps and not get credit for them?"

"I know." I grinned. "Silly, huh? But it keeps me working toward a goal. I'll just run out and check the car."

"Do you want me to go with you?"

"No need." I shook my head.

Pulling a light jacket over my pajamas, I slipped down the stairs and out the front door, quietly unlocking the dead bolt. The fall evening was a bit cool and made me wish I'd gotten re-dressed rather than taking the shortcut of throwing on a jacket.

Walking to where we'd parked, I unlocked the Jeep and reached behind the seat. Sure enough, it had simply slipped to the side and I'd missed it when we arrived.

As I shouldered the bag and started back to the house, I took a deep breath. I was really looking forward to this weekend and couldn't wait to get started on the new project. Staying in the beautiful B and B was an added bonus. The night air was scented with crisp leaves and some flower I couldn't quite identify. I raised my gaze to the sky.

Oh, wow.

When you're in a city, or even in a small town like St. Ignatius, where I live, you don't get the full impact of a dark night sky in the country. With the absence of artificial light, the cosmos was sprinkled with millions of tiny lights.

Not watching where I was going, I stumbled over something in the grass and nearly fell.

Righting myself and getting my bearings, I looked toward the house. As my eyes focused, I noticed a figure in the shadows near the side of the building. The figure moved quickly around the corner and disappeared. There wasn't any reason someone shouldn't be out walking around, but still I felt a prickle of unease on the back of my neck. Maybe it was just being in a strange place and the fact that the area was so isolated, but it made me hurry my steps a little.

I slipped back into the house and quietly shut the door, relocking the dead bolt. The quiet was broken by a sharp, high-pitched bark. Probably Colette's little dog. I hoped she was settling down for the night and wasn't planning on staying up, because she'd already irritated a few people at dinner.

I meant the dog, of course, but the same could be said for Colette.

Not wanting to be the cause of any further commotion, I made my way up the stairs as quietly as I could.

Carefully opening the door and creeping into the bedroom, I carried my cosmetics bag to the bathroom and set it on the counter.

"Did you find it?" Dixie asked from the bed, where she was already wrapped up in the soft covers.

"Yes, I did."

"Now you can finish getting ready for bed without worrying about missing out on those steps." Dixie rolled back over. "Good night."

"I'll try not to make too much noise," I said to her back as I flipped the switch on the bedside lamp by my bed. "Will this light bother you?"

I waited for her to answer, but all I got was a soft snore. Though we'd never shared a room, it didn't surprise me that Dixie was one of those awake-then-out people who could fall asleep almost immediately. I, unfortunately, did not drift off so easily. Hanging up my jacket, I plugged in my activity tracker and finished getting ready for bed.

Propping up several pillows, I settled in and reached for a mystery book I'd just started. After a couple of chapters I felt my eyelids getting heavy.

Closing the book, I turned out the light and snuggled under the quilt, thinking about all the tasty dishes we were going to collect for the Arbor family cookbook.

Chapter Two

I hadn't set an alarm on the small clock by the bed, but I had set one on my phone for six-thirty. As it turned out, neither was needed, as I woke up at six o'clock on my own. Dixie was sound asleep, so I quietly brushed my teeth and pulled on my running, aka walking, clothes.

I could take care of my early-morning steps and have a jump-start on the day before breakfast.

The house was quiet, though I thought I could hear someone moving around in the kitchen, and the smells coming from that direction promised something tasty for the morning menu.

Opening the door and stepping outside, I looked around. I was a little afraid to try the road that led to the B and B because it didn't have a wide shoulder and I didn't want a run-in with a car. The Arbor House property covered several acres, according to Gwen, so I figured I could trek the area behind the house without trespassing on someone else's property.

I headed to the back and started a brisk walking pace. The grass was a bit damp from morning dew, but the temperature was nice, and it was so relaxing to keep moving without any interruptions. I'd been walking in the mornings for the past month and, unless I was really early, most of my neighbors were up. Don't get me wrong, I love living in a small town and knowing my neighbors, but stopping to chat really messes with my ability to get all my walking in.

The backyard couldn't really be called that. At least not as it related to most backyards. It was more like a park. The big green expanse was broken up only by the archery range and the pickleball court. Gwen had explained pickleball to me yesterday. I hadn't realized the paddle sport was so popular. It looked like fun. Maybe Dixie and I would get a chance to try it out. I wasn't sure I'd be any good, but running after that ball would certainly up my step count.

Not that I was obsessed with my steps.

I had just completed my circle of the area near the court and started toward the archery range, when I heard a bark and saw a streak of white out of the corner of my eye.

Oh, no.

It looked like Colette's little poodle had gotten loose and was running around the area off leash. There were probably dozens of things she could be getting into that she shouldn't. Things much worse than eating chocolate mousse.

I tiptoed in her direction.

"Come here," I called.

She stopped and tipped her head to one side as if she didn't quite understand.

"Come. Here." I tried again. Maybe the dog only understood French. I tried to think whether I knew any French that would be helpful. My vocabulary, unfortunately, was limited to being able to adequately order in a French restaurant and didn't include calling a dog.

"Come, sweetie," I coaxed as I continued toward her, searching my pockets to see if I had anything that might serve as a treat to coax the dog to me. Or at least something that might look like a treat. Normally, I wouldn't be so devious in tricking the poor pup, but if she headed for the nearby woods at best she could end up covered in brambles, and at worst she could get attacked by a predator.

As I got closer, I could see Frenchie was technically not off leash. The bling-studded pink tether was still attached but trailing behind her as she ran to-and-fro. She spotted me and ran toward me and then, as I reached down to grab her, she took off.

"Okay, you trickster." I ran after her. Okay, more like a really fast walk.

Frenchie circled back, darting past me in the other direction. Goofy dog. At least I'd be racking up steps on my tracker. Again, not that I'm obsessed.

"Come on, come here." I patted my leg.

She headed back toward the archery targets and I followed. Stopping behind one, she barked again. I hurried forward, thinking I could grab ahold of the leash and as I did, I tripped over something and fell to the ground, skidding across the grass. There went my pristine new exercise pants.

What on earth had I stumbled over?

Stunned by the impact, I slowly opened my eyes.

Sightless violet eyes stared back at me; perfectly platinum hair was matted with blood. She must have hit her head when she fell. But I didn't think it was the head wound that had killed Colette.

I was pretty sure it was the arrow sticking out of her chest.

My own heartbeat pounded in my ears.

I struggled to stand and to comprehend what I was seeing.

I tried to scream but couldn't force any sound around the lump that had formed in my throat. Once on my feet, I snatched up the now-still dog and took off.

At first in the wrong direction. As my senses returned, I corrected course and ran as hard as I could toward the house.

Opening the first door I came to, I ran directly into Jonathan Arbor.

"There's—it's—Colette." I pointed toward the backyard. "Behind the tar—" My brain couldn't come up with the words to explain, but my tone of voice must have conveyed the urgency.

J.J. stepped forward, and I realized all the siblings were gathered in the lower-level sunroom.

"What's wrong?" Jezzie asked, grabbing my arm.

"Hurt," I said and pointed again.

All three shot out the door and toward the archery range. I sat down in the nearest chair, still holding Frenchie, who nuzzled into the crook of my arm as if she too was shaken.

I don't know how much time passed before they came back, but one look at the solemn faces told me I'd been right. Colette was dead.

"Let's get you upstairs." Jonathan helped me up from the chair. The sunroom stairs led to a deck off the back of the house, which unfortunately overlooked the back of the house and gave a clear view of the archery range. Someone had covered Colette with a blanket.

It didn't matter. Sightless violet eyes and blond hair tinged with blood were etched into my memory.

I turned to the group who had followed behind Jonathan and me. "I'm just going to go upstairs and change."

Climbing the stairs, I suddenly realized I still held the poodle.

When I opened the door to our room, Dixie was propped up on the bed, leafing through the Arbor House cookbook we'd worked on. She stopped mid–page-turn.

"I was about to come looking for you." She looked me up and down. "What happened to you? And why do you have the dog?"

I tried to set the poodle on the bed, but she was having none of that.

"Colette is dead. Shot with an arrow. Out there." I waved my hand in what I thought was the general direction of the back of the house.

"What?" Dixie jumped up. "Are you okay?"

"No." I felt my lip quiver. "I'm not. I went for a walk, and it was still kind of dark and Frenchie here was running around, and I tried to catch her and tripped over Colette."

I took a gulp of air and sat down on the bed.

"She had an arrow sticking out of…" I tapped my chest.

"Jeepers." Dixie sat back down. "It's too early for anyone to be on the archery range. And what would she have been doing out there anyway?"

"I think maybe taking this one for a walk." I nodded toward Frenchie, who still was stuck to me like glue.

"Here, let me take her so you can clean up and change." Dixie held out her hands.

I tried to hand over the dog, but she resisted, finally yielding and letting Dixie take her but not without a whimper of protest.

I grabbed a change of clothes and entered the bathroom. Washing my face and changing into clean clothes helped a bit. Applying a bit of makeup added some color so I wasn't quite so pale. I quickly ran a brush through my hair and stepped back into the bedroom.

"Better?" I asked.

"Yes. Not that you looked bad." Dixie held Frenchie against her, petting the dog's head, but the pup struggled to get to me as soon as she spotted me. "I think you've got a friend here."

"She's probably traumatized by what happened to her human." I picked her up and she immediately tucked herself back into her former position.

"I imagine." Dixie shook her head. "Suppose we'd better head downstairs and see what's happening. I assume they called the police."

"I didn't wait to find out."

Closing the door behind us, we could hear voices from the main floor. Once we'd reached the bottom of the stairs, it was clear the family had assembled in the living room.

"Would you like some coffee?" Gwen appeared with a cup and a carafe of coffee.

"Oh, yes, please." I accepted the cup and held it out so she could pour. Frenchie shifted so she didn't lose contact with my side.

Gwen turned toward Dixie, holding out a cup.

"No, thank you."

"There's also tea." Gwen pointed toward a tray that sat on the walnut library table. "Or other things to drink in the kitchen. Just let me know what you'd like."

"Tea will be fine." Dixie moved toward the table.

An awkward silence followed me as I juggled the dog and my coffee, and made my way toward the couch.

"Where are they?" Jezzie looked at her watch. "We called them over twenty minutes ago. It's a good thing this wasn't an emergency."

"Let's stay calm." J.J. held up his hands. "The dispatcher said they were tied up at an accident scene and would get to us as soon as they could."

I took a sip of my coffee and looked around the room. Everyone was present. Jezzie and Tom, J.J. and Lucinda, Jonathan and Gwen. Wait—where was Theo? I wondered who'd had the awful task of breaking the news to him. Probably his mother or father. I was sort of rooting for Tom. Maybe Jezzie had a softer side but, if so, I hadn't seen it yet.

Dixie joined me on the couch. "You know we're still in Jameson County, right?"

"No, I did not know that," I whispered. That meant that the investigator would be a county sheriff that we knew all too well.

It seemed like hours passed, but it was probably only minutes. The atmosphere was tense and a bit odd. How could it not be?

Jezzie, a doer, was definitely having trouble sitting still. Her foot-tapping was about to drive me crazy. Tom, her husband, seemed oblivious to it. But then my impression had been Tom was most of the time unaware of what was going on around him. It looked like he might be using the time for a quick nap.

J.J. paced back and forth, sat down by his wife, got back up. Lucinda had some papers in her hand and periodically jotted notes. Gwen had told me Lucinda was a former history professor before she had gotten into doing genealogy. She'd promised to mention my interest to Lucinda in case she could share some tips. Maybe she was taking advantage of the waiting to catch up on some of her research.

Gwen busied herself with making sure people had beverages and Jonathan flipped through messages on his phone.

I got up and refilled my coffee cup from the carafe Gwen had left on the table.

* * * *

I watched out the window as the Jameson County sheriff's car pulled into the parking area. Sheriff Terry Griffin got out and J.J. walked out to meet him. The two men talked as they approached the house, and soon I could hear the front door open and close.

"Your sheriff is here," I whispered to Dixie.

She didn't say it, but gave me the *not my sheriff* look. It was an ongoing ribbing between us and maybe inappropriate, given the circumstances. But somehow the slip into something routine and normal helped me deal with the awfulness.

The sheriff walked into the room, looked around at the assembled group, and came to a full stop when he spotted the two of us.

"I'm Sheriff Griffin," he introduced himself to the rest. "I'm sorry for the delay and for your loss." He paused for a moment. "I'm going to have a look outside and then I'd like to talk to everyone, so if you wouldn't mind hanging out here for a few more minutes, I'll be right back."

"This way." J.J. gestured toward the hallway that led through the kitchen and to the back porch.

"Just a second." The sheriff turned back to the group. "When was the last time anyone saw…" He glanced down at his notes. "Colette?"

"She was gone when I woke up this morning." Theo stepped in from the hallway. Apparently he had been close by. "I didn't think anything of it though because I just figured she'd taken Frenchie out."

"Frenchie?" the sheriff asked.

"Yes." Theo nodded toward me. "Her poodle."

"Ah." The sheriff gave me a nod and then turned to follow J.J. down the hall.

The subdued group hadn't needed to be asked to stick around; it didn't seem like anyone was interested in going about their day.

"When I get a chance to talk with Gwendolyn, I'll ask what she'd like us to do." I leaned in to speak in a low voice to Dixie. "The family may prefer that we give them some privacy."

"Whatever you decide is fine by me." She shifted on the couch. "If they want to postpone the whole project, we'll make it work."

"We've got a couple of things in the works." I absently patted Frenchie's head. "The Diamondback Lake Community cookbook is almost done, and the other one with the Ladies' Aid group is just getting started. We should be able to reschedule this if that's what they want to do."

Dixie nodded agreement.

Hilda had brought coffee and blueberry muffins for everyone earlier and now she was making the rounds, refilling cups and collecting plates.

Quiet and efficient, she moved from person to person without interrupting the conversations. Her salt-and-pepper hair was cropped close to her head, a pixie cut, my stylist would have called it. But there was nothing pixie-ish about Hilda. Though she wasn't a large woman, she had what I would call a solid build. Arms that could lift a tray of empty dishes or mash a mess of potatoes. Strength gained from hard work, not a workout at the gym. I wondered what she thought of the siblings and if she'd known any of them as kids. And what her take was on Colette's death. Sometimes the people in the background are great observers. My musings were interrupted as Jezzie jumped to her feet.

"Be careful, Mother." She hurried to the stairs as Marta made her way down slowly.

Jonathan moved across the room and offered her his arm. He escorted her to an easy chair close to where I was sitting near the fireplace. More importantly, away from the window.

"Mother Arbor, can I get you a coffee or tea?" Gwen offered as her husband got his mother settled.

"Thank you, dear." Marta eased back into the chair. "I would have a tea if it's not too much trouble."

"No trouble at all." Gwen headed off to the kitchen.

Jezzie said something to Theo I couldn't quite hear.

"Jezebel Rebecca Arbor, I'm old but I'm not feeble. Nor am I hard of hearing." Marta glared. "Yes, I do know what's going on. Not that anyone bothered to tell me directly."

I wasn't sure whether we were talking about the dead fiancée or something else, but the tension between mother and daughter was palpable. And believe me, I'm an expert on mother-daughter tension.

"Terrible business this." The older woman turned toward me.

"It is," I agreed.

"I understand you found her."

I nodded.

She started to say something else, but Sheriff Terry was back and ready to talk with the family. He took a spot in the middle of the room.

"I'm going to want to talk to everyone individually. Most of the interviews won't take very long. The coroner is on his way, along with a crime scene team, so I'll have to ask you to stay away from the backyard for now."

"A crime scene team?" Theo paled. "You think someone meant to kill Colette?"

"We don't know at this point," Sheriff Terry explained. "That's why we need to take a cautious approach and be careful not to destroy any evidence that might help us figure that out."

"It is deer season," J.J. commented.

Deer season? I looked at Dixie. I didn't know a lot about hunting, but it didn't seem to me to be likely that Colette had been mistaken for a deer.

"Not ruling out the possibility," the sheriff responded. "Could have been a hunter with terrible aim. Early-morning light makes it hard to see and your property is right up against the woods. Lots of hunters this time of year."

J.J. shrugged. "Whatever you need from us."

"Mind if I set up at a table somewhere?" Sheriff Terry asked.

"No problem." Gwen was back with tea for Marta. "Come with me." She took him through to the dining room.

The oak table, where just last evening everyone had been eating and joking, seemed alien now. While I didn't like the idea of Colette being shot by an inept deer hunter, I liked even less the idea that there might be someone who harbored the intent to kill her.

That would take quite a bit of skill, though, wouldn't it? I wasn't sure I could hit the target on the archery range, let alone a moving target.

The sheriff stepped back into the room. "I've finished setting up and am almost ready to talk with everyone. If you could just bear with me for a few more minutes." He crooked a finger in my direction. "Sugar, come with me."

I stood and stepped toward him, still holding Frenchie, who'd decided I was a permanent sleeping spot.

"Leave the dog with Dixie, Sugar."

If anyone in the family was surprised we were on a first-name basis with the Jameson County sheriff, they didn't show it. I handed Frenchie off to Dixie and followed Sheriff Terry. He went through the kitchen and out the back of the house.

"I'd like you to walk me through finding the victim." He nodded toward the archery range. "What were you doing wandering around so early?"

"I've been trying to exercise more." I pointed at the step-tracker on my arm. "I'd gotten up early and thought I'd get a walk in before everyone was up and about."

"You and Dixie are doing a cookbook for the Arbor family." We trudged across the grassy area, now dry, toward where I'd found Colette.

It wasn't a question, but I nodded. "They asked us to come for the weekend get-together so that we'd have a chance to meet everyone and maybe collect some stories to add to the cookbook. I think the family members are staying all week."

It was one of the things I loved about the community cookbooks we published. While the main part of the book was the recipes, there was usually an opportunity to sprinkle in some background and include some things that would personalize the cookbook. That was true whether it was for a town, a group, or in this case a family.

In the community cookbook biz, the story was the project. And in this case the story was not just about the memories of good food growing up: Food was the family's business.

"What?" I suddenly realized that the sheriff had been asking me something while I'd been letting my mind wander. Trying not to think about beautiful Colette and how awful she'd looked when I found her.

"What caused you to notice the victim?"

"I didn't at first." I cringed at the memory. "I tripped over her."

I explained to Sheriff Terry about noticing Frenchie, trying to chase the dog down, and then finally tripping over Colette and landing beside her.

"I grabbed the dog and ran for the house."

"You then told the family members and they came to check it out." He continued walking, hands in his pockets. "They were all up and dressed for the day, then?"

I nodded. I couldn't remember exactly what everyone was wearing, but I thought they'd all been dressed.

"They were in the downstairs sunroom." I pointed back at the house. "It felt a bit like I'd interrupted a family meeting. None of the spouses. Just J.J., Jezzie, and Jonathan."

"J.J. said they were discussing their mother's health and the fact she's still living on her own," he said, and slowed as we approached the now-cordoned-off area where I'd found Colette.

"She does seem frail," I noted. "Though it seems like she's got all her faculties." I thought about her comments this morning. If she had an inkling they were having that discussion without her, that could account for her sharpness with Jezzie.

We stopped before we got to the area that was now protected with stakes in the ground and crime scene tape strung from one to the next. Colette's body was thankfully covered with a blanket.

"Do you think it could be hunters?" I looked up at Sheriff Terry.

"It's possible," he answered, his gaze shifting to the surrounding woods. "But if so, we still could be talking involuntary manslaughter. No one should be hunting in this area. The area to the west is part of a nature preserve and the north part belongs to a neighboring farmer."

I'm not good with directions, so the west-north distinction was lost on me, but what I did understand was that there should not have been hunters in the area.

"Sheriff?" A deputy was headed toward us. "It looks like the shed where they keep all the archery equipment has been broken into."

Sheriff Terry started to walk away and then turned back to me. "You can go on back to the house."

"You don't need anything else from me?"

"I know where to find you." He nodded in dismissal and then joined the deputy.

As I walked toward the majestic Victorian, I glanced at the time on my step-tracker. It was then I remembered seeing someone when I'd gone out to the car the night before. Or at least I'd thought I saw someone. I made a mental note to mention it to the sheriff the next time I saw him.

When I got back to the house, it seemed the subdued group from earlier had morphed into a flurry of activity while they waited.

Jezzie had apparently given everyone tasks. She had Dixie sorting recipe cards at the dining room table.

I joined her just in time to hear Jezzie say to Theo, "What do you mean, you don't know how to contact her family?"

"They weren't close," Theo bit out. "I think they live in the Twin Cities, but I'm not sure."

"The sheriff is going to need that information."

"I know." Theo walked out.

I thought she could have been a little more sensitive in her approach. Her son had just lost his fiancée, after all.

Sidling up beside Dixie, I looked at the piles of handwritten cards she'd placed on the tabletop. "What can I do?"

"I could use a glass of water and a marker." She looked up. "I've got the categories separated but I keep getting mixed up about which pile is which.

"Be right back." I approached Jezzie and asked about markers.

"In the desk drawer in the kitchen." She pointed in that direction.

When I entered the kitchen, at first, I didn't notice Theo standing by the counter. He seemed lost in thought and didn't act like he'd heard me enter. Not wanting to startle him, I cleared my throat to let him know I was there. He still didn't move.

"Hello," I said, walking nearer in hopes he'd see me.

"Oh." He straightened and shook his head as if clearing it. "Sorry, I didn't know anyone else was in here."

"I'm looking for a glass."

He pointed at a cupboard.

I opened it and took down a glass and paused. "I'm sorry for your loss."

"Thank you." He wiped his face with his hands. "I still can't believe it."

"Had you been engaged long?"

"Just this week." He took a deep breath and looked up. "I did the whole big pop-the-question very publicly."

"Billboard? Skywriter?" I asked.

"Not quite that publicly." He smiled for the first time. "I planned a romantic dinner at one of her favorite restaurants with the engagement ring in a fancy box anchored by a red rose."

Ah, I would have guessed him a romantic.

I walked to the sink and filled the glass. "How did you two meet?"

"At a charity event." Theo's shoulders drooped. "We both came with other people. I suck at those types of functions and was counting the minutes until I could leave. Colette introduced herself to me, and we hit it off right away."

"I'll bet she was comfortable at the event." I set the glass down and leaned on the counter.

"Why do you say that?" He turned his head to look at me.

Oops. I hadn't meant to offend.

"Just that she seemed to be very outgoing."

"Yes, very outgoing." He choked up.

"I'm sorry. I shouldn't have asked."

"No, it's better to talk about her." He blew out a breath. "My family members apparently are going to simply pretend she never existed."

A wave of sadness washed over me for Theo, so alone in his grief.

"Is her family in Chicago also?"

"No. Well, I don't know." He raked a hand through his dark hair and paused. "I really don't know."

I waited, not wanting to press, but thinking about what I'd overheard earlier between him and Jezzie.

"She was estranged from her family," Theo continued. "They hadn't spoken in years. She didn't say what happened, but it must have been big."

"That's too bad." I picked up the water glass, opened the desk drawer, and located the markers. "I'm sure that Sheriff Griffin can help you with contacting them."

"Yeah, I guess." He frowned. "Though I'm not sure they will care. She made it sound like they hadn't had contact for quite a while."

"I hope that's not the case." I patted his arm. "Again, my condolences."

Carrying the water and markers back to the dining room, I thought about what could have caused Colette to have been estranged from her family. In my experience, family riffs don't have to be over big issues. Or at least they're not always. Misunderstandings can begin over something small and grow into family members taking sides and not talking to each other.

That's often the key, isn't it? Communication, or rather lack of communication. When people stop talking to each other. At least that had been the case with my parents. The beginning of the end of their marriage wasn't the fights, though as a kid I'd dreaded those. It was the silence between them. As an adult, I understood those dynamics better and realized it wasn't that simple. But it kind of was. When we stop communicating in a relationship, we've given up.

I took the water to Dixie and handed her the markers. I wanted to tell her about my conversation with Theo, but with most everyone still in the room I couldn't. I'd have to fill her in later.

While I'd been in the kitchen, Sheriff Terry had returned and begun his interviews with the family. It appeared that J.J. had been first on the list and now Jezzie was up.

I picked up one of the handwritten recipe cards. "These are priceless. Do you think they'd let us use some of them in photos for the cookbook?"

"I don't know why not." She added one to the desserts pile. "Most of them are amazingly legible."

In just a matter of minutes, Jezzie was back and Jonathan was tagged for a chat with the sheriff. He hadn't been kidding when he'd told them it wouldn't take long.

Dixie and I cycled through the remaining recipe cards and the sheriff cycled through the rest of the family members. Dixie was the last one called and I knew her statement would be brief.

She returned in just a few minutes, the sheriff following close behind.

Such a great couple: Sheriff Terry solid and steadfast and Dixie good-natured and caring. Though fiery at times. I still didn't know the whole story, but had recently learned a little more. They'd been an item in high school and then due to some drama and misunderstanding they'd spilt. Dixie had married someone else. To all accounts a nice man who she'd lost a few years ago to a farm accident. Terry had moved away and only recently returned to the area. Years had passed and yet there were still remaining hurts from whatever had happened between them. They sorted it out enough so that recently they'd decided they could be friends. I thought it could be a lot more, and I wasn't alone in rooting for romance. If they would just talk.

See what I mean? The key is communication.

Sheriff Terry thanked the family and again expressed condolences.

"I'll be in touch with any new information from the forensics team." He headed for the door and then turned back. "Dixie and Sugar, would you walk out with me?"

Chapter Three

We stepped out onto the porch and into a day that had gone from cool fall morning where you needed a jacket, to hot Indian summer where short sleeves and shorts would be more in order.

"Did either of you talk with the victim last night?" he asked.

"There wasn't time," I responded. "She and Theo arrived and there was the dog incident and then everyone scattered after that."

"The dog incident?" The sheriff stopped walking.

I described what had happened with Colette and Frenchie.

"After that we all went to bed," Dixie added.

"And you didn't hear anything after that?"

"Well, Sugar went outside to look for her charger in the car." Dixie pointed toward my Jeep.

"What time was that?" he asked.

"I think around ten-thirty or so." I hadn't checked the time to know for sure.

"Did you see anyone while you were out here?"

"I wanted to mention that to you—I did see someone. Or thought I did, anyway. There was someone near that east corner of the house." I pointed at where I'd seen the shadowy figure.

"That's north." Dixie shook her head.

My sense of direction is sadly lacking and often finds me lost. I'm thankful to whoever it was that came up with GPS navigation. Otherwise I'd be lost even more often.

"Right." I shrugged. "I couldn't see very well, it was so dark, and they were gone very quickly."

"Could it have been Colette?" the sheriff asked. "Maybe walking her dog?

"I suppose it could have been, but not walking her dog. When I got back to the house, I could hear Frenchie barking from somewhere inside." I guess that didn't necessarily mean that Colette was in the house as well, but it seemed like she and the dog had been inseparable.

"I'll have the team take a look there." He squinted into the sun. "How much longer are you here?"

"Just through the weekend," Dixie answered.

We'd arrived at the Jameson County Sheriff's Department vehicle.

"If you think of anything, let me know." He opened his car door and climbed in. "You have my number."

We turned and headed back to the house. Dixie's face was already pink from our time standing out in the sun.

"You're going to need some sunscreen, lady, if you're going to spend any time out in this," I noted.

She touched her pink cheeks. "The curse of being a redhead. I don't think I packed any. Why do you think Terry thought we might have any information on Colette?"

"I think wishful thinking on his part. Theo was in the kitchen when I went to get the markers for you and I talked with him a little bit. He truly has no contact information for Colette's family."

"None?"

"He 'thinks' they might be from the Minneapolis–St. Paul area."

"Wow." Dixie stopped walking. "I can't imagine agreeing to marry someone without meeting their family. Strange."

"It is," I agreed. "But then, not everyone stays close to home like you. Look at me. I've lived in several states."

"But still, if you were to get serious about someone, you'd want them to meet your mother."

"Maybe." I wasn't absolutely sure about that. Although, meeting Cate Sugarbaker might be the true test of a guy's mettle.

"Do you think it could have been hunters?" I kind of wanted for it to be hunters. It would still be sad, but it would be accidental.

"It's possible." She shaded her eyes and looked at me thoughtfully.

"But not probable?"

Dixie shrugged. "There are a lot of requirements for bowhunting and some strict safety measures, but people can be stupid. There was a story in the news a while back about a guy that was killed when a boulder went through his windshield. He was on the interstate and some kids threw it off a bridge."

"Wow, you never know how much time you've got." I sighed. "You're driving along, minding your own business and *pow*."

We were quiet as we continued walking back to the house. What a strange turn the weekend had taken.

When we entered the house, it appeared everyone had scattered to their own pursuits. The intent of our staying the weekend had been so we could collect recipes and talk with the family about what they wanted in the Arbor family cookbook. With Colette's death, they might not want to continue.

"We should probably talk to the family and see what they want to do?" I walked through the dining room and looked out the window. The crime scene team was packing up their equipment and Colette's body had been removed from the scene.

"Whatever they decide is fine with me." Dixie walked over to the area where she'd been sorting recipes and began stacking the file cards.

"I'll go see if I can find Gwen, since she was our contact on the project." I looked around. No one was in the living room. Maybe the kitchen.

At the massive island, Hilda was prepping for lunch. A gingham apron wrapped around her stocky body, she was cutting up veggies and stacking them on a tray like she was a contestant on *Chopped.*

"I'm looking for Mrs. Arbor," I explained.

She turned and gave me a questioning look.

"Sorry. I'm looking for Gwendolyn Arbor," I clarified. I'd forgotten there were three ladies with that title.

"She's working in the office right now."

"And the office is…?"

"Back there." Hilda pointed with her paring knife.

For the first time I noticed a short hallway beyond the pantry. Hoping it was okay to interrupt, I followed it to a small office area that looked a lot like my office back at Sugar and Spice Cookbooks.

"Hello." I stopped in the doorway and Gwen looked up. "I hope I'm not interrupting."

"A welcome interruption." She smiled. "I'm just catching up on some bill paying. Have a seat." She indicated a chair across from the desk.

"I wanted to talk to you about the cookbook project and continuing the weekend." I stepped in and sat down. "With the situation being what it is, we absolutely would understand if your family wanted to postpone the project."

"I hadn't thought about that possibility." She looked thoughtful. "I guess I should ask what they want to do."

"No pressure." I didn't want to make them feel like we were bailing on them. "Dixie and I simply wanted you and the rest of the family to know that we are good with whatever the decision is. If you'd like, we can pack up and head out this afternoon or if you'd prefer, we can stay. Entirely up to you all."

"Sugar, I appreciate your thoughtfulness." Gwen moved a file and leaned back in her chair. "I suspect they'll want to go ahead, but let me take the temperature of the group."

"That sounds good." I moved to stand.

"An awful situation." Gwen sighed.

I sat back down. "It sure is."

"And how awful for you to find Colette," she noted.

I nodded. No need to mention that Colette was not the first dead body I'd encountered. "Did the sheriff give you any indication of what they're thinking?" I asked.

"They found that the shed where all the archery equipment is stored had been broken into."

"Do they think vandals, then?" That would make more sense. To me, at least.

"The forensics team that they sent wasn't sharing much information with us, but from what J.J. got, they dusted a bunch of areas for fingerprints," she said. "Of course, several of the family members' fingerprints will show up. They've been all over the property since they arrived."

"This was the original Arbor family homestead?" I gazed around the room and wondered what its original use had been. I thought I'd understood from the conversation last night that this was where the siblings had lived as children.

"It was." She bit her lip. "When Jonathan and I took it over it wasn't in great shape. It had sat empty and neglected for several years."

"There must be a lot of shared memories, then." I was always a little envious of shared memories, having no siblings myself.

"Yes, Jonathan has a lot of great childhood stories about living here. I think that's where his love of restoring these old homes came from."

"When did the family move?"

"When the business got going, they moved to a bigger, more modern home up north, closer to the factory. Their mom still lives there, but I think they'd all like to see her downsize."

"I'm interested in telling the story of how they went from a cherished family recipe for quiche to mass-producing the Arbor family's frozen dinners that we find in the grocery stores. I know that's not what they've said they're looking for in terms of the cookbook, but it's a great way to preserve the family history."

"Mother Arbor would be the one to tell that story." Gwen bit her lip. "I don't know if she's willing or not. Most older people want to talk about their past, but she tends not to do that. Plus, as you might have noticed, she's a bit frail."

"I hope she'll consent, but it's your call."

"Really the Arbor family's call," Gwen pointed out.

"Right." I rose. "Once you've talked with them, let me know how the family feels about continuing with the project. I'm going to go see how Dixie's coming with those recipes."

When I walked back through the kitchen, Hilda was on the phone and didn't notice me.

"I can't make the payment today," she said in a low voice to whoever was on the other end. "I'm working at the Arbor House; I'll have to get it to you on Monday."

I guess, as Dixie and I said earlier, we all have our own stuff to deal with and you never really know what someone else is going through.

Dixie was still at the dining room table, finishing up her notes on the recipes. "So many wonderful recipes," she said. "We've got plenty of material, at least in terms of recipes, if they decide to move forward. What's the word?"

"I talked to Gwen, and she'll discuss with the rest of the family whether they want to continue and let us know." I helped Dixie gather up the recipe cards, stacking them carefully, making sure to maintain the sorting Dixie had done.

"Sounds good."

We were kind of at loose ends until we knew something, and I was going a little stir-crazy. What I'd loved about the B and B when I first visited was how isolated it was. The perfect getaway. Today, what I didn't love about it was how isolated it was.

When Dixie needs to think, she cooks. When I need to think, I eat. Which had never been a problem for me until lately.

"How about we take these upstairs and then go for a drive?" I suggested. "When I was here before I just drove to the house and then back home. Matilda wasn't up for any side trips."

Dixie shook her head. "I can't believe you named your GPS lady."

"It seemed like since we spend so much time together, we should be on a first-name basis."

"You're crazy." She laughed.

"I know."

We dropped the recipe cards and Dixie's notes in our room, and I grabbed the keys to the Jeep. I didn't want to disturb Gwen again, but didn't want the family wondering where we'd gone, so I popped into the kitchen thinking we could let Hilda pass on the message. She was nowhere to be found.

I wrote a note and left it on the dining room table. I didn't think we'd be long, but it seemed rude to disappear without telling anyone.

"For having so many people in the house, it sure seems deserted," I commented as we climbed in the Jeep.

"It's such a big house." Dixie fastened her seat belt. "And so many separate areas that make it perfect for its current use."

"I sort of feel bad about disappearing, but it didn't seem right to disturb them."

"Houseguest rules for when there's been a murder weren't covered in your Southern manners class?" Dixie smiled.

"Do you think it's really murder?" I'd been afraid to say too much when we were within earshot of the family, so it was a relief to be able to talk without looking over my shoulder.

"I guess I'm leaning toward accidental death," Dixie answered. "But I have to tell you, while you were in talking to Terry there was a lot of discussion among the family about business and very little of it about Colette. Seems a bit cold, given the circumstances."

"You can't think one of them killed her."

"As Sheriff Terry says, everyone's a suspect." Dixie raised a brow.

"Well, I think we can eliminate a few of them," I argued.

"Like who?"

"Theo, for example," I said, holding up a finger. "Why would he bring Colette to the family get-together to kill her? Besides, he seems genuinely heartbroken over her death."

"And I don't think Marta is up to the job," Dixie added. "Two off the list."

"I'm still going for accidental, but seriously, even if they had the opportunity, where's the motive for any of them?" I stopped at the end of the drive. "Which way?"

Dixie pointed and I turned right. Which I'm not sure was east or west… or for that matter north or south. But I was almost sure it was the opposite of the way we'd come when we arrived, because the mailbox was on my left this time.

We traveled for a bit down the road. It was paved but very narrow, which was why I'd been reluctant to consider leaving the property for a walk. Even in the interest of getting in my ten thousand steps.

Unlike many of the roads, this one was not bordered by fields, but rather trees and bushes that grew near the pavement. The area was somewhat hilly, but just soft, rolling hills and the leaves of the oak, walnut, and maple trees had begun to turn colors, but only slightly. There was a palette of green with the promise of autumn crimson and gold mixed in.

"Look—there's an old cemetery." Dixie pointed at a gate I'd almost missed seeing. "Let's take a look."

Lilac Hill Cemetery, the metalwork over the wrought-iron gate proclaimed.

I turned in and Dixie hopped out and opened the gate.

After driving through, I parked on the grass, as there wasn't anywhere else to go, and I didn't want to block the entrance.

"Are you sure it's okay I leave the car here?" I put the Jeep in *park*.

"It will be okay." She looked around. "There aren't any other options."

The small cemetery was well maintained. Flowers and flags dotted the landscape. There were definitely many more old headstones than newer ones. I wondered, since Arbor House had been the family home, if some of the family might be buried there.

"You'd think since it's called Lilac Hill that there'd be lilacs, wouldn't you?" I mused.

"Those are lilac bushes." Dixie pointed at a bank of green shrubs against the fence line. "They don't bloom this time of year."

"Oh. I knew that." I'd grown up in apartments and condos, so I had a spotty education where plants and yards were concerned. I was learning to take care of a yard, but often found I had a lot to learn. Much to my next-door neighbor's chagrin.

We walked through the stones, looking at the inscriptions. Some were weathered and hard to read but most, even the ones from the 1800s, were in decent shape. One good-sized stone said *Jules, Famous White Mule, Served in the Civil War, died March 1888.*

"I didn't know you could bury mules with humans," I commented as I continued down the same row.

"Very few rules in the old rural cemeteries." Dixie followed. "Very few records as well."

"That's what I'm afraid I'm going to run into with trying to find my father's family." I came to the end of the section. "Hard enough when you have records to go on, but I have very little."

"Take a look at that." Dixie pointed to a marker that stood taller than the rest, an obelisk with urns on each side filled with flowers.

I approached. *Joseph Arbor, Beloved Husband, Devoted Father*, it said. It gave his birth and death dates and then there was a spot for Marta that already had her name and birthdate, the date of death obviously having been left blank.

It gave me a shiver. "How would that make you feel? To have your name already on a gravestone?" I ran my fingers over the blank part of the marble stone.

"Kind of creepy." Dixie moved closer. "Those flowers look fresh, so someone must visit fairly frequently."

"There doesn't seem to be other family members nearby." I looked around. "Maybe Joseph senior was the first to settle in the area."

"Only a few others. The cemetery is so tiny." Dixie stepped carefully among the gravestones. "Look at how old these stones are."

There were two small stones with the names Sallie and Sarah. Their year of death was noted as 1847.

"Some sad stories behind these, I bet." I touched the top of the stone nearest me. "That must be before Iowa was even a state, right?"

"I don't remember my state history for sure, but I think we became a state in 1846, so around the same time." Dixie ducked as a bee who'd decided to befriend her buzzed around her hair "Are you ready to head back?"

"I am." I nodded. "If this side trip was supposed to cheer us up, I think it missed the mark."

Dixie nodded her agreement.

"Sampson, Brooks, Huston." I read off some of the other names as we made our way back to the Jeep.

We climbed in and I turned the Jeep around in the grass and then headed out onto the roadway.

"You've turned the wrong way to get back to Arbor House." Dixie pointed.

"I have? Shoot." I checked the rearview mirror to see if I could make a U-turn. "I don't like how narrow the road is. I think I'll drive a little farther and see if there's a better place to make a turn."

"It is pretty tight." Dixie looked out at the side of the road.

There wasn't much of a shoulder beside the road and the ditches looked deep. Traveling a mile or so—in the wrong direction—we spotted a widening up ahead. A former gas station had been turned into a little shop. I pulled into the driveway and started to make the turnaround.

"Since we're here, let's grab something to drink," Dixie suggested. "I'm parched."

"Now that you mention it, I am too." I parked the car and we went in.

"Hi there," a voice called from the back. "Be with you in just a minute."

"No problem," Dixie called back. "We're just after something cool to drink."

We headed for a refrigerated case against the wall that held a variety of drinks. I picked out a water and Dixie a lemonade.

"Hello." A smiling elf in men's clothing spoke from behind us. We turned and he held out his hand. "Nice to meet you. Name's Shorty."

Of course, it was. Toy George, the lady who ran the Red Hen Diner in St. Ignatius, was short, but this guy had her beat. Like her, he had thick white hair, though a lot less on his head. His sprouted out of his ears and above his eyes. I wondered if they were possibly related.

"Is your last name George?" My thought slipped out before I could stop myself.

Dixie gave me a look, like I'd lost my mind.

"Nope, last name's Gentry. My brother's name is George, though. Does that help?"

"It's warm out today." Dixie obviously thought changing the subject was a good idea. "We needed a cool drink."

"Yep," Shorty agreed. "Not quite fall; we've still got some summer left. Hope these warm days don't stir up bad storms."

Dixie reached in her bag and pulled out some bills. "How much for both?" She nodded toward the bottles of water and lemonade I held.

"Let's see. Those are one and a quarter, so two-fifty plus tax." He walked toward the antique cash register that sat on the counter: A beautiful piece with dark polished metal and a very ornate design. It looked heavy and I wondered if it was left from when the building had been a gas station.

Dixie handed him three dollars and he turned to a more modern machine behind him. Apparently the antique cash register was only for show.

"Don't believe I've seen you here before." Shorty handed her back her change. "You from around here?"

"No, we're from St. Ignatius. So not too far away." She tucked the coins in her purse.

"We're staying at the B and B, Arbor House," I offered as I handed Dixie her lemonade.

"You are!" His shaggy eyebrows shot up. "Heard there'd been a girl killed there this mornin'."

Bad news traveled fast. I often said in St. Ignatius the grapevine was faster than any news source, but I hadn't expected that in such a rural area.

"Unfortunately, that's true," Dixie confirmed. "She was visiting the Arbor family."

"Shot with an arrow, I heard." Shorty leaned toward us.

"Hmm." I didn't want to lie and say we didn't know, but it didn't seem right to add to the gossip.

"That's okay, if you don't want to talk about it." He reached over and patted my arm. "If I were looking into what happened, I'd be giving that whole bunch a lookie-loo." Shorty reached up and rubbed his nearly bald head. "Yes, I would."

"Why is that?" Dixie asked.

"They're all champion archers, that's why." He nodded. "Yes, they are. Champions. Every last one of them."

Chapter Four

Dixie and I walked back to the Jeep and got in. I sat for a few minutes in silence before starting it, thinking about what Shorty had said.

"I don't even know what I think about that." I looked over at Dixie. "Even if several of them had the ability, there's still no good reason why."

I started the car, turned around, and this time headed down the road in the right direction. We drove in silence. Both lost in our thoughts.

Like I'd said earlier, if this little side trip had been supposed to cheer us up, it had been a major fail.

When we pulled into the long drive at Arbor House, the place still looked as tranquil and quiet as when I'd first seen it. At the time, I'd wanted Dixie to see it as well and this weekend had seemed like the perfect opportunity.

Now, I was thinking about what might be hidden behind a beautiful facade and the idea that one of the members of the Arbor clan might be responsible for a young woman's death.

* * * *

While we'd been gone, everyone had reassembled and lunch was being set out in the dining room. We washed up and joined the family.

"I thought since we'll probably do a full dinner tonight that we'd go with something light for lunch." Gwen helped Hilda carry in the trays of food. "I hope that's okay."

We were missing a few of the family members. It seemed J.J. had gone for a drive himself and Jezzie had taken a tray to her room to do some work. Theo wasn't feeling up to lunch and who could blame him? I wondered about Frenchie, who Theo had taken from Dixie earlier when Sheriff Terry had arrived. Grand-mère Marta was also having lunch in her room.

The menu was a tasty cream of asparagus soup, tossed green salads, and a crudités platter with three different dips. My favorite was a spicy hummus dip, but the ranch and fresh dill dips were good as well. I'd have to see if Hilda would be willing to share the hummus dip. I wanted these recipes for sure.

Jonathan engaged Dixie in a discussion about St. Ignatius and the community. He was restoring a farmhouse not far from our town and she knew the family that had lived there.

Lucinda had printed out some basic information for me on genealogy because, true to her word, Gwen had mentioned my interest in researching my father's roots.

As soon as everyone was served, Gwen joined us at the table.

She settled into her chair and picked up a carrot from the platter. "Before we get too involved in chatting or get done and take off in different directions again, I wanted to tell you two that we discussed whether to continue the family cookbook project. And the answer is, yes. We want to go forward."

"We are pleased." I looked at the group around the table. "We certainly would have understood if you had wanted to postpone, but we are happy to continue."

"I second that." Dixie spoke up. "We're so sorry for your loss and understand this is a difficult time. We'll do our best to collect what we need without disrupting your time together."

"We appreciate your offer to delay, but this is really the best time to catch everyone together." Lucinda looked up from her soup.

With that good news, we could spend the afternoon sorting through the recipes we needed and reviewing the list with the family members to make sure they were okay with what we had planned. If we could get the list approved before we left, we'd be well on our way to assembling the recipes and moving on to the next steps.

Lunch was finished and cleared quickly, leaving us the use of the dining room table for our work.

Dixie had already done a great job of sorting the recipes and so we spent some time culling through them and discussing the mix of dishes. Even though a family cookbook leaves a little more leeway, you still want a good variety.

By the time we'd been at it for an hour, I was stiff from sitting too long and also parched.

"Shall I go see if I can find us some water or tea?" I rose and stretched out my arms.

"That would be great." Dixie laid aside her notebook. "I think we've got enough to work with, but maybe we should take some extras to swap out if we need to. I do wish we had more of a feel for whether any of these are special to the family."

"I'll be right back." I headed for the kitchen.

Hilda was stirring a pot of sauce on the big commercial stove.

"That smells good." I inhaled. "Something yummy planned for dinner?"

"A pasta buffet," she replied. "Three different pastas, three different sauces."

I was beginning to understand that running a bed-and-breakfast wasn't just about the having a big beautiful house and serving great food. It was also about planning interesting menus and giving your guests options. Gwen certainly had the creative knack and Hilda seemed to be the perfect partner to making it happen.

"I'm sorry to bother you." I stepped to the side so I wouldn't be in her way. "Dixie and I were wondering if we could get a couple of glasses of water."

"Deserted you, have they?" She gave the sauce another good stir and then turned down the heat.

"Well…" I paused, not wanting to criticize our hosts. "It's okay. We just thought they'd be spending more time hanging out with each other and talking."

Hilda shrugged. "Just because you have the same last name, doesn't mean you have anything in common."

Wisdom that was probably all too true. I thought of my own family. Sometimes I wondered if I had anything at all in common with my mother and her sisters. My father's side? I had no idea.

"What's your last name, Hilda?" I didn't know that I'd heard anyone say.

"Gentry," she said as she turned back to the stovetop.

"As in Shorty?" I asked. What were the odds?

"The very same." She didn't look at all surprised. "He's my brother. I gather you met him."

"We did." I looked at Hilda with new eyes, not finding any traits they shared. Physical traits, at least. "But, you're…"

"Not short?" She raised a brow.

"Not as short as your brother, anyway."

"Adopted." She went back to stirring the sauce.

"My father was adopted." I leaned against the counter. "I don't really know anything about his birth parents."

"Families aren't always about birth. Sometimes you're born to them, sometimes you create them." Philosopher Hilda was back.

"There's iced tea and lemonade in the big refrigerator." She pointed with her spoon. "Glasses are in the cupboard next to the sink."

I got down two glasses and poured an iced tea for me and a lemonade for Dixie.

Carrying them back to the dining room table, I thought about what Hilda had said.

I'd had such an interest in finding out about my father's birth parents, I hadn't really examined why.

The afternoon flew by and soon it was time to clean up for dinner. Dixie and I packed up our things and headed upstairs. I was really looking forward to the pasta buffet after smelling the sauces simmering in the kitchen.

We both changed into something a little nicer for dinner—Dixie a lime green shift that had a darker green shrug. And me, a deep burgundy sundress I'd recently bought on an infrequent shopping trip. I was wishing for a sweater to throw over it, as my arms were pasty white. Too much time indoors this summer.

* * * *

The pasta buffet was the perfect arrangement as everyone arrived in the dining room at different times. I wondered, not for the first time, if the family realized how much work Gwen had put in to make this a nice gathering. It wasn't just closing the bed-and-breakfast for the time they were here—it was also supplying meals and other amenities for the whole family.

There didn't seem to be much interest in pitching in and helping. J.J. and Jezzie were wrapped up in business things, Lucinda was buried in her research, and everyone seemed to have something to do.

"This is a great idea," I said to Jonathan, who was seated beside me.

"Gwen's idea." He lifted a forkful of penne pasta to his mouth.

"It was nice of you two to open the house to the family and we really appreciate you including us in this weekend." I twisted fettucine around my fork.

"And what a weekend it's turned out to be." He raised a dark brow.

"Yes." I took a bite. "That's for sure."

"Are you doing okay?" he asked. "Finding Colette like that must have been a big shock."

"It was." And one I didn't really want to dwell on. "I'm doing okay."

"I'm sorry we've just sort of left you and your partner to figure things out on your own."

"It's not a problem. We've sorted through a lot of recipes today."

"Well, good." He took a sip of wine. "Still, we should have been a little more attentive."

"You were a stockbroker before moving back to Iowa, right?" I remembered his background from my first meeting with Gwen.

"That's right."

"And now back here and working with your siblings on the business?" I knew he was more into restoring houses, but assumed he also had a role at Arbor Family Foods.

"Oh, no." He waved a hand toward the group. "I leave all that to J.J. and Jezzie. They've been at it so long, there's no place in it for me."

Gwen and Dixie joined us and the talk turned to recipes. We hadn't had any of the ones from tonight's meal in what we'd reviewed so far. Gwen promised to look and see if there was anything written down, or if these were perhaps ones that had been verbally handed down.

Once everyone was fed, Gwen began gathering plates and cleaning up the buffet area. Jonathan got up to help.

"Is there anything at all that we can help with?" I asked, getting up also.

"No, we've got it." He didn't seem to mind the lack of pitching in from the rest of the family.

Gwen swung by, her hands full of dishes. "There's a gorgeous full moon tonight. You and Dixie should grab a glass of wine or beverage of your choice and sit out on the front porch for a bit."

"I'd feel so much better if you'd let us help with the dishes and cleanup."

"Very little to do." She smiled. "We'll stack these in the dishwasher, hit the button, and be done."

With the refusal to accept our offer of help, Dixie and I decided to take Gwen's advice and enjoy a little time on the porch. There were several chairs scattered across the decking. The night air was nice, not too cool, and the moon was—as promised—full and bright. We each took a chair.

"Wow, I wish I could paint," I said. "Or like Max, take photographs."

Max was the photographer we worked with on our cookbook projects. And Max and I were… Well, I wasn't exactly sure what we were. We were still figuring that out.

"I'm not sure it can be captured." Dixie leaned back and took in a deep breath.

We sat like that for a while, enjoying the quiet. The sounds of the chatter from inside the house seemed distant. Eventually it got chilly and we decided it was time to turn in.

"I'll take our glasses to the kitchen." I held out my hand for Dixie's glass. "You go on up."

"Okay." She handed it to me. "You're going to wash them, aren't you?"

"Probably." She knew me too well. I didn't like the idea of leaving them for someone else and it would take very little time.

* * * *

When I got back to our shared bedroom, Dixie was propped up, leafing through a cooking magazine. Not my idea of bedtime reading. I was more of a mystery or thriller fan. Besides, if I started reading about food, I'd probably gain weight in my dreams.

"What took you so long?" she asked. "Did you get lost?"

I'd known she would ask and I didn't want to, but I was going to have to fess up.

"No, I wanted to get in a few more steps, and so I walked around the driveway a little bit. I'm still a little freaked out about going any farther, but it's pretty light with the full moon and I figured I was safe enough there."

I pulled out my charger and plugged in my phone. Checking my fitness-tracker, I could see it needed charging too, so I plugged it in as well.

"Your dedication is impressive." She laid aside the magazine. "I wish I had that much willpower."

"My mother usually called it pigheadedness, which I don't think she meant as a compliment, but I'm pretty sure I got it from her." I grinned. "But here's the interesting thing: You won't believe what I saw while I was out walking."

"I probably won't."

"I had started back to the house when I noticed I was only fifty steps away from my ten-thousand-step goal. I went back to the parking lot and circled around the cars and was almost there. Then I noticed someone in that same area where I saw the figure last night."

"And?" Dixie prompted. "Could you see who it was?"

"I don't know what possessed me, but I went toward where the person had been."

"You did what?" Dixie sat up, causing pillows to tumble to the floor.

"I know." I shook my head. "That was stupid. But anyway, when I got to the side of the house no one was there. I didn't stick around, but I'm going to go back and look at that area in the daylight and see what's there that someone would be lurking two nights in a row."

Gathering my things and heading to the bathroom to change, I stopped and turned back to Dixie. "Maybe there's an innocent explanation."

A sharp bark, followed by a growl, echoed from somewhere in the house. Theo had his hands full not only dealing with Colette's death, but also her pooch, who did not seem to be his fan.

Earlier, I'd almost offered to let Frenchie sleep in our room. I was sure Dixie wouldn't mind. But I'd been hesitant to interfere, and I'd thought the pup might be some comfort to the guy.

From the sounds of it, I might have been wrong about that.

Chapter Five

Sunday morning the sun shone through the gap in the drapes in the guest room, hitting me right across my eyes, the rays heating the side of my face. Hopefully that meant some warmth was in store for the day.

I should have set my alarm and been outside and logging some steps earlier, but I have to admit I simply couldn't make myself do it. The memory of finding Colette was too vivid.

I could have walked in another direction. Or taken a few laps up and down the long driveway, but I was still a bit freaked out that someone, either accidentally or with intent, had shot an arrow that had killed her. I didn't want to be the second victim of an ill-trained or untrained hunter.

Dixie was already up and in the shower when I woke up. She dressed while I showered and then waited while I threw on some khakis and a sweater. I might need something lighter as the day wore on, but for now the soft knit was perfect for the brisk coolness of the morning. As we headed downstairs, the smells from the kitchen filled the house with warmth and goodness.

Gwen was in the dining room, cup of coffee and her computer by her side. She looked up and smiled when we entered.

"Multitasking. Trying to be with friends and family and catch up on some emails," she noted. "You know how that goes."

"Boy, do I ever." I was the one who kept up with the business correspondence at Sugar and Spice Cookbooks and though we didn't get as much email as I was sure Arbor House did, it took daily handling. I had brought my laptop along for the weekend so I didn't get behind.

"We're opting for a sort of a help-yourself buffet this morning." Gwen pointed toward a sideboard that had been laid out with warming dishes. It definitely worked for their family get-together that the bed-and-breakfast was set up to accommodate feeding guests at different times. "Please help yourselves."

I didn't have to be told twice. Dixie and I each picked up one of the beautiful china plates. Spode was my guess. It reminded me of a Buttercup Spode pattern my Aunt Celia had: Dishes we used only on special occasions in the Sugarbaker family. Carefully balancing the plate, I spooned on some scrambled eggs, added fresh fruit, and picked out a piece of tasty-looking multigrain toast.

I was deciding on a scale of one to ten how rude it would be to take a slice of banana bread in addition to the toast when Lucinda entered the room. Okay, full confession—I'd already taken it. I was actually deciding how many more steps I'd need to clock to offset the banana bread.

"Good morning." Lucinda looked around the room, but no one other than Dixie and I looked up. Picking up one of the china plates, she joined us at the buffet.

"How are you doing?" I asked, sliding the thick slice of banana bread on my plate.

"Not too bad, considering," she responded, looking over the spread. "Has Mother Arbor been down?"

Dixie shook her head. "We've not seen her."

I was looking forward to checking out the elderly lady's frame of mind. I had really hoped for some time with her to put some context around a few of the recipes. Given that she was frail and the family members were very protective, I was willing to do our chats in small doses if that would help.

Dixie and I carried our food to the big table. A centerpiece of fresh flowers in vivid fall colors set off the gleaming oak.

Lucinda filled her plate and joined us. And I have to say, she'd not been shy about multiple choices in the carb department.

"Isn't this breakfast lovely?" she asked, taking a bite.

I hadn't tasted any of mine yet, but if it tasted anything like it smelled, it was more than lovely.

"Who does all your baking?" Dixie asked. "Whoever it is, they do a great job."

"The multitalented Gwen actually does some of it. Though I have no idea where she finds the time. But Hilda, who you met when she was helping out with serving the other night, does most of it."

"She has a real talent." Dixie took a bite of the cinnamon-apple muffin she'd picked up.

"Hilda begins with a basic muffin recipe we discovered in the family recipe box as a base and then you can make endless variations," Gwen offered, looking up from her computer. "She has tried some interesting combinations."

We ate in silence for a few minutes, enjoying the tart apple and warm spice flavors.

There was a thump on the stairs as Theo trudged down, clutching a pink dog carrier and looking like he hadn't slept more than a couple of winks.

"Good morning. Grab some breakfast." Lucinda pointed toward the buffet.

"I mostly need coffee." Theo rubbed a hand across the stubble on his chin.

As he did, I noticed a bright orange Band-Aid on his thumb that hadn't been there before.

"Did you get hurt?" I asked, afraid I already knew the source of the injury.

"The little pooch and I aren't doing so well together." He held up the bandaged digit. "I thought things might go better if I fed her one of those fancy treats Colette had always given her. She got all excited and in trying to get it out of my hand, she nipped my finger."

"Has she been out this morning?" I asked.

"No, not yet." He set the carrier on the floor. As he did, there was a small *woof* from inside.

"I'll take her out for you," I offered. I'd finished all of my food except that slice of banana bread I'd been saving for last.

"Go for it." Theo ambled to the coffee service, poured a cup, and took a long sip.

"Any luck in contacting Colette's family?" Lucinda asked.

"None." Theo sat down at the table. "I reached out to some of her friends from work, but they didn't have any information. They suggested calling the human resources office at the company where she worked. I'll call tomorrow when they're open and have them check her emergency contact info."

"That seems like a good idea." Lucinda took another bite.

I was wishing I hadn't been so quick to volunteer to take Frenchie out. I was afraid I'd miss out on any other news. Theo seemed in a sharing state of mind this morning.

I coaxed Frenchie out of the carrier and snapped her leash on. Dixie started to get up.

"You go ahead and finish your food." I motioned her to sit back down. "I'll just pop out with Frenchie here and be right back." I tried to telegraph that she should stay put and listen in for the latest news.

Frenchie seemed excited to get out of the house, and we took a quick walk down the side of the parking lot so she could do her business.

Once we'd done our loop, I walked Frenchie toward the area where I'd thought I'd seen someone that past two nights. There were huge green hostas and big blue hydrangea bushes planted along the side of the house, and a slight dip in the elevation at the back.

Stopping at the corner, I looked around, careful to keep a grip on Frenchie's leash. We walked the area. I don't know what I expected, but there was no evidence of anyone having been hanging out by the house.

The flowers on the hydrangea bush were a sweet floral and I leaned into inhale the scent. As I did, I noticed a cigarette butt on the ground at the root of the bush.

Thinking DNA and identification, although a secretive smoker was not necessarily a killer, I didn't want to contaminate the evidence. Leaving it in place, I hurried back to the front of the house.

We were headed back to the entrance when a car pulled into the drive. Stepping onto the grass to make sure the pooch and I were out of the way, I watched the dark blue Buick pull forward into a parking place.

J.J. got out and pocketed the keys, heading for the house. Had he not even seen me?

Frenchie and I followed on his heels as he climbed the steps to the front porch and then went inside. Opening the door, I kept Frenchie on the leash, not sure if I could trust her to roam free or not. And for that matter, I wasn't sure what the house rules were about pets.

I stopped to slip off my shoes. I'd collected a bit of grass clippings when I'd moved off the parking lot surface and into the grass.

J.J. dropped the car keys on a small table and continued on.

The group in the dining room greeted him and Gwen pointed him toward the food.

"Were they able to find the problem?" Lucinda asked.

"They were and the brakes are now as good as new," J.J. answered. "Though it may be time to trade. I think that car is jinxed."

"Now, almost everything is fixed." Lucinda smiled. "It's almost new."

"Any news?" he asked Theo as he passed by him on his way to get a plate.

"None." The guy looked a little more pulled together than he had earlier. But either being more with it or his uncle's presence seemed to have made him less talkative.

"Good morning, Mother Arbor." Gwen set aside her laptop and stood. "Would you like some breakfast?"

She moved forward to take Marta's arm as the older woman made her way slowly down the staircase. J.J. set his plate aside and came forward to help.

"Mostly I need coffee." The octogenarian echoed Theo's earlier sentiment. Her sharp dark eyes surveyed the room as J.J. and Gwen helped her cross to one of the easy chairs near the table. Her gaze landed on Frenchie.

"What are you going to do about that dog?" She turned her head to look at Theo. "I could hear her whimpering late into the night."

I hadn't heard the pooch, but Marta's room was probably on the second floor and closer to Theo's room.

"We're still trying to track down Colette's family." Theo poured a cup of coffee and took it to his grandmother. "I hardly slept at all."

"No luck with her friends?" Marta asked.

Theo looked at her over the rim of his cup. "None."

She reached over and patted his hand. "We'll sort it out."

I wasn't sure what that meant, but it was clear the matriarch of the family doted on her grandson. And, unlike his mother, she didn't blame him in any way for the tragedy.

Gwen had put together a plate for Marta and set up a small table for her use. Theo stayed near her side and they talked quietly. He coaxed the poodle back in her carrier and closed the door.

The family members who'd been there for breakfast seemed ready to scatter and I wasn't sure what the plan was for the day. I had finished my coffee and enjoyed that slice of banana bread, which was worth every single calorie, by the way.

I wanted to be sensitive to what they were going through, but on the other hand they'd asked us to continue with the project.

Leaning over to Dixie, I said quietly, "I need to run back to our room to make a phone call. While I'm there I'll grab that packet of cover samples that Liz sent us." Liz was a local graphic designer we'd used on most of our cookbooks. She always managed to somehow understand the overall essence of a project which has a huge impact on the finished product. For the Arbor family project, I felt like she'd nailed it. I hoped they thought so, too.

"Good idea," she agreed. "Maybe we can get a few decisions out of the way, and then if they'll let us take the recipe cards with us, we can get out of their hair."

"It's worth a try." I gave her a thumbs-up.

Chapter Six

I met Hilda on the stairs on my way to our room to pick up the cover samples.

“That poodle seems to like you,” she commented.

The woman carried a small tote of cleaning supplies and took the stairs slowly, one step at a time. “Maybe she could stay in your room, instead of with Theo,” she continued. “Then she won’t cry all the time.”

“I feel bad for her.” I followed Hilda up the stairs. “It’s got to be confusing to a dog that the person she’s most attached to is suddenly gone.”

“Imagine so.” She shifted the tote to her other hand.

“Do you clean the rooms as well?” I asked. “I thought from what Gwen said, you mainly help with the baking and occasionally with the serving. That banana bread was amazing, by the way.”

“That’s one of my recipes.” She almost smiled. “Simple. Turns out every time.”

“It certainly turned out today. I confess I snuck a second piece.”

“Glad you liked it.” Again, not quite a smile but a small twitch at the side of her mouth told me she was pleased at the compliment.

“So, if you’re not cleaning…” I left off the rest of the statement, hoping she’d fill in the blank.

“Police are done with Theo’s fiancée’s room.” She nodded down the hallway. “Gwen’s busy. Theo’s a basket case. I told them I’d take care of packing up the girl’s things.”

“That would be hard.” I hadn’t thought about Theo having to deal with packing all of Colette’s things. And what would they do with them when they hadn’t identified any family members. “Would you like some help?”

“Suit yourself.” She shrugged.

That wasn't a no, so I followed her down the hallway. Hilda opened the door and I stepped in behind her.

The police had either left a mess when they went through the room or Colette had been a bit of a slob in the short time she'd been there. Clothing was draped over the bed, the brocade fainting couch, and even the lamp. Hilda located a suitcase that had been stashed in the closet and laid it open on the bed.

I plucked the purple silky robe off the chaise, carefully folded it, and placed it in the suitcase. Hilda started on the closet, taking things off the hangers, folding them and adding them to the suitcase.

Theo had never mentioned what Colette did or where she worked, but looking at some of the labels, it was clear that she'd had expensive taste. Some of the brands were ones I hadn't shopped even when I'd been part of the corporate world. Some of the scarves she had undoubtedly cost more than my whole wardrobe. And then there were the shoes. Not sure how many pairs you need for a weeklong stay at a rural bed-and-breakfast, but Colette had made sure she had any situation covered. And, to top it off, there were six purses of various colors and sizes.

I was sure the police had checked pockets and bags when they'd searched the room, but I couldn't help but pat down jackets and sweaters and peek in purses as I went. All empty. It looked like if they'd found anything, they'd taken it with them.

The bright pink coat Colette had worn when she arrived had slipped off its hanger and fallen on the floor of the closet. Hilda pulled it out and shook it. And then laid it aside.

I picked it up. "I can't help but think if she'd been wearing this coat that she might have been more visible. And maybe would still be alive." I reached out and patted the coat, checking the pockets. "I wonder why she chose a different jacket."

"Not even a different one of her own. Though she had plenty." Hilda waved a hand at the growing stack beside the suitcase.

"What do you mean, not her own?" I asked, picking up yet another scarf and doubling it over.

Hilda had moved on to the dresser, opening the top drawer. "She must have gotten downstairs and then realized she needed a jacket. Then I guess she may have taken one from the hooks by the back door," she explained over her shoulder.

"Oh, no." I stopped mid-fold.

I didn't know that the pink coat would have made any difference at all, but it seemed sad that a split-second decision to borrow a coat that blended in with the landscape could have cost the poor girl her life.

In addition to Colette's luggage, a pastel pink case embroidered with Frenchie's name held doggy toys and grooming items. I set it by the door. What would happen to poor Frenchie was still up in the air. I held out hope that a dog-loving family member would be found, but in the interim, Theo might be able to use some of the dog toys. It was clear the guy didn't have a lot of experience with dogs.

I helped Hilda get the suitcase closed and off the bed. We placed it along with Colette's matching train case of jewelry and cosmetics by the door.

"Thank you." She dropped to the end of the chaise, eased off one shoe, and rubbed her foot. "It was easier with help."

"You're welcome." I patted her shoulder. "I'm happy to make myself useful."

"What's next for you and your friend?" she asked. "I hear they want to go forward with the cookbook."

"They do, but I'm having trouble getting them to focus." I suddenly realized how that sounded. "Sorry. Don't get me wrong. What happened was awful and it's understandable everyone is thrown for a loop. Who wouldn't be, right?"

"Don't worry." She shook her head. "I know what you mean. But they would have been unfocused even without this. That's the way they are."

"You've known the family a long time, then?" I sat on the edge of the bed.

"A long time ago when we were all kids. We were in school together." She continued to rub her foot. "Then the Arbor food business hit the big time and they moved away. I was glad to see this place taken on by some of the family. Jon and Gwen have fixed it up real nice."

"How did you come to work here?"

"I retired from teaching a couple of years ago and moved back to the area. I'd been looking for something part-time. A teacher's retirement only goes so far."

"And you're a great cook," I added.

"Gwen needed some help in the kitchen when they first opened, and a neighbor told her I might be interested."

"And they remembered you?" It seemed possible. Though Hilda looked older, if they were in school together, they might remember.

"Not at all. Jon was younger than me and was pretty little when they moved away."

"How about the older siblings?" I asked.

"No. J.J. has always had his head in the clouds even as a kid. Jezzie was a year behind me in school, and I guess we really didn't hang out with the same crowd."

"Hmm."

I was still disappointed they didn't remember Hilda. I'd moved around a lot so I hadn't kept in touch with anyone from my childhood, other than cousins. But I'd always imagined if you had roots in a place that it would be different.

"Doesn't bother me." She reached down to put her shoe back on and winced.

"Are you okay?" I asked. "That looks painful."

"It's fine. I have a bad corn." She tugged the shoe on. "It gives me fits from time to time. I should've worn different shoes."

"Can I help you lug these somewhere?" I pointed at the suitcases.

"No, Gwen said just to leave them here."

"All right then, I'm headed up to my room to get the paper samples and we'll see if I can corral enough Arbor family members to make a decision on the cover." I winked at her.

"Good luck with that." This time it was a real smile.

* * * *

Climbing the stairs to the third floor, I considered Colette and her personal belongings. The fact was there'd been not much personal in what we packed up. Was that because the forensics team had taken anything personal when they searched her room? Or was it that Colette herself was a bit of a mystery?

I called Sheriff Terry's number and left him a message about the cigarette butt I'd discovered by the house. I wondered if I should put it in a baggie or something, but decided I'd wait for him to call me back.

Pulling the bag of materials from where I'd stashed them under the bed so they'd be out of the way, I dumped them out on top of the quilted spread. Sorting them out, I selected the cover samples and a few of the paper samples to take downstairs with me.

We'd planned to have this discussion with the family group the first day of our stay, but yesterday had, as my Aunt Cricket would say, gone to hell in a handbasket.

The day seemed to be warming up, so I swapped my sweater for a cotton top, ran a brush through my hair, and touched up my lipstick.

"Straighten your shoulders, suck in your stomach, put some color on, and get to it!" I said to myself in the mirror.

That one was not from Aunt Cricket; it was directly from my mama. Classic Cate Sugarbaker.

Picking up the samples, I started back downstairs. When I reached the second floor, I heard a door open. I was sure someone had just gone in the room that had been Colette's. I stood for a few minutes, waiting to see if they would come back out, but everything was quiet. Stopping outside the door, I listened, but couldn't hear anyone moving around inside.

I waited a few more minutes, but decided I couldn't lurk in the hallway any longer. Taking the stairs, I reached the first floor, where Dixie was engaged in a conversation with Lucinda about family farms. Dixie's family had been in farming for several generations and Lucinda had come across background during research of her own family that suggested they might have been part of early farm settlements in Iowa.

Lucinda got up to refill her coffee and Dixie leaned toward me. "What took you so long?"

I glanced around. Everyone else had gone except for Jonathan, who was flipping through photos on his iPad.

"Sorry. I helped Hilda pack up Colette's things," I whispered. "I thought there might be some clues there, but it looks like the forensics people took anything like that."

"That because it's their job." She bit her lower lip. A sure sign that she wanted to say more. "Shall we see if the group is up to even talking about the cookbook?"

"I'll track down Jezzie and Gwen." I put my packet of materials on the table. "You see if you can keep Lucinda and Jonathan here."

"Got it." She reached for the samples.

Gwen had disappeared since I'd been upstairs, but now that I knew where her office was, I knew where to look. The kitchen was empty, so I slipped down the short hallway. She was at her desk, but on the phone.

She held up a slim finger.

I waited while she finished the conversation and then explained what Dixie and I were looking for in terms of decisions about the finished product. We'd talked about it before we'd taken on the project but it had been a while, and I didn't know how much information she had shared with the rest of the family. She'd been our point person.

"I think I can round up the family members." She stood. "Or least the ones that have an interest in the cookbook. I'm afraid Tom is only interested in his golf game or his futures. And Theo—well, poor Theo is understandably focused on other things."

"Of course," I said. "I hope asking to get these decisions out of the way isn't inappropriate. We don't want to push."

"Oh, no, not at all." She picked up her cell phone and dropped it in the pocket of the gauzy jacket she wore. "We could use something else to talk about right now.

"I'll meet you in the dining room with everyone I can track down."

"Sounds good." I headed back to the dining room.

Dixie had managed to hang onto Lucinda and Jonathan. I cleared newspapers and random glasses from the table and laid out the cover papers and some examples.

"I'm told I need to be here." Jezzie walked in from the kitchen entrance and looked over the items on the table.

J.J. was right behind her. He took a pair of glasses from his pocket and joined her in perusing the cookbook materials.

Gwen came from the other doorway. She must have been looking for the others.

"That's all of us for now." She touched flushed cheeks. "Theo is resting and Mother Arbor said to get started without her. She'll join us in a little while."

No one even mentioned Tom, so I guess it was a given that he wasn't part of the decision-making team.

Usually we try to narrow the field on potential covers, taking the advice from our graphics guru, Liz, that too many choices were overwhelming for most people. In the case of the Arbor family project, I'd taken Liz's field of ten and knocked it down to eight potential covers.

They were laid out on the table in no particular order.

"We can eliminate this one right away." Jezzie picked up a very stark modern design and moved it to one side.

"I agree." Gwen nodded. "It doesn't fit with your brand at all."

"I would think simple would be good." J.J. moved to the other side of the table to look at the design Jezzie and Gwen had rejected.

"Shows what you know," Jezzie replied a little too sharply. "The Arbor Family Foods look is down-home, family, loyalty, simplicity."

"But this is for the family," Lucinda noted in defense of her hubby. "It's not a corporate cookbook."

"Are you saying the family isn't also those things?" Jezzie plucked a different cover design from the group. "I like this one."

She had picked one of the busier covers, with graphics of cooking and baking utensils behind the title. It did have the down-home feel she'd mentioned.

"J.J., I like your idea about a simple look and feel," Jonathan chimed in. "But I agree with Jezzie that we need something that's warmer. More family-like. How about this one?" He held up another sample.

Jonathan had nailed it. At least in my opinion. The one he'd pulled out was the cover I would have picked for the Arbor family cookbook. It was classy and simple, and yet had warmth and elements that spoke to home cooking.

Looking around at the group, I saw mostly nods of agreement. I moved the other covers off to the side.

"What do you think, Mother?" Jezzie turned toward the stairs where Theo held Marta steady so she could navigate the stairs.

The two approached the table. I grouped the selection of covers so they could both see. I'd thought we had a cover, but maybe not.

"I like that one." Marta pointed a thin finger at the one Jonathan had picked a few moments ago. "What do you think, Theo?"

"I like it." Theo smiled at the older woman. "You have good taste."

Okay, maybe we were still on track.

"If you go with that cover"—I pulled out a couple of compatible interiors—"this would be the type of inside pages we'd be looking at."

I placed the examples by the cover and shoved the rejected covers out of sight.

It didn't take long for the group to come to a decision on the inside pages. They were a decisive bunch. Though it was clear they deferred to Marta, which was only right. After all, she and Joe, Sr. had started it all.

As soon as the decisions were made, everyone scattered. Perhaps with things to take care of, or off to do whatever they'd been doing before we rounded them up. You'd think since they didn't get to spend time together normally that they'd use this get-together to hang out with each other. I was finding out my fantasies about warm and fuzzy family dynamics were not completely on the mark. Families are complicated, I guess.

"I'm going to run these back upstairs." Dixie held up the pile of samples. "So we don't lose track of what was selected."

"Sounds good." I thought they'd made some good choices.

I found myself alone in the room with Marta.

"Is it odd having all your grown children under one roof?" I asked. "I'll bet it's been a while since that happened."

"Hmm." She picked at imaginary lint on the skirt of her dress.

One more thing before I lost my chance. Or lost my nerve. Here goes nothing.

I took a deep breath. "I'd really like some time to talk with you before we leave."

Her head raised up and her dark eyes met mine. "About what?"

"We like to include some family stories when we do this type of cookbook," I explained. "Maybe a story about where you got a particular recipe. Or a memory about making it for a special occasion."

"Doesn't sound very interesting to me." She scooted back in her chair.

"Trust me, it's more interesting than you think." I smiled at her. "It would only take a few minutes."

"Okay." She shrugged. "I'm going upstairs to rest now, but maybe after. Would you find Theo for me?"

"Absolutely." I stood.

Dixie had returned and I asked if she'd seen Theo.

"No, I haven't," she said. "Do you want me to check around for him?"

"He's probably gone back to his room." Marta pointed toward the stairs. "You'll be able to find it by listening for the whiny dog."

Okay, then. Clearly not a Frenchie fan.

"I'll check." I climbed the stairs and sure enough, all it took was a walk along the corridor to identify which room he and Frenchie were sharing.

I tapped lightly on the door.

I could hear him say something, probably to the dog, and then the door eased open. "Yes?" His dark hair was tousled and his usually crisp clothes were wrinkled. Maybe he'd been trying to grab a nap to make up for his lack of sleep.

"Your grandmother would like some help in getting back to her room," I explained.

"Oh, okay." He straightened his shirt and ran a hand through his hair. "No problem."

He followed me downstairs where Marta was talking with Dixie.

Approaching her, he leaned in and gave his grandmother a kiss on the cheek. "Ready to take a rest, dear heart?"

"More than." She smiled up at him.

He helped her up and crooked an arm. She took hold and they made their way toward the stairs.

"If you're ready for that talk after you've rested, just let me know," I reminded. I didn't want her to forget that she'd given me a semi-commitment.

Dixie waited until they were all the way up the stairs before she asked, "What was that about?"

"You know, I'd been wanting some family stories to sprinkle in with the recipes and we're not getting anything like that at all."

"No, I'd hoped there would be more exchange between the family members." She stood.

"They all seemed reluctant to ask their mother about talking to her. So, I took the opportunity while everyone else was out to ask her if she'd be willing."

"Aren't you the sneaky one?" Dixie grinned.

"I just think she's not quite a fragile as they all think she is," I said quietly. I felt guilty questioning the other family members' judgment, but I did believe she was tougher than they thought.

"Let's go for a little walk."

Dixie gave me a quizzical look. "Are you short on steps?"

"Now that you mention it, I am." I glanced at my step-tracker. "Come on."

Once we were outside, I told her the real reason I'd wanted to get out of the house. Explaining about walking around the house while I'd been out walking Frenchie and finding the cigarette butt in the bushes. The bushes that were in the area where I'd seen someone lurking, not once, but two nights in a row.

"Do you think it could have been someone who followed Colette here?" she asked.

"I don't know what to think." I shrugged. "I called the sheriff and left a message."

"Okay, so now I'm a little creeped out about staying here." Dixie shivered. "I'm kind of glad we're leaving this evening after dinner."

"I hear you," I agreed as we headed back to the house. "Let's get our business taken care of and then we'll be out of here faster than two shakes of a lamb's tail."

"I don't know how fast that is, but I'll be ready." Dixie looped her arm with mine.

Chapter Seven

Back in our shared room, we packed so that we'd be ready to leave after dinner. I made sure to pack my charger so I didn't leave it behind. Looking around at the room, I thought about what a difference a day made.

Gwen had let us know that dinner would be ready at six o'clock. In the interim, I kept thinking Marta would send word she was ready for our talk, but she didn't. In fact, she didn't even come down for dinner. Gwen explained the older woman was having a tray in her room. So much for my victory in getting her to agree to talk with me.

The family had arrived in the dining room at the appointed time, trickling in one at a time. I still found it amazing that Gwen and Jonathan had managed to create the perfect atmosphere for a bed-and-breakfast and still keep the feel of a family home. The warm, rich furnishings, the polished wood floors, and the solid, well-placed antiques all merged to create a luxurious, yet homey feel.

Gwen's advertising painted the B and B as a setting with tranquility and relaxation, and up to yesterday, I would have agreed. For the first time I wondered whether having a death occur on the property would affect her business.

Tonight, the fare was simple: prime rib, roasted rosemary potatoes, fresh green beans. Simple didn't mean it was unremarkable. The food was perfectly done and mouthwateringly delicious.

However, it was difficult not to contrast the sober mood with the dinner from two nights ago. Still a beautiful setting and great food. The wine still flowed freely and it appeared Jezzie might have again had a wee bit too much. But this was not the chatty and animated group from the night we'd arrived.

Hilda had helped Gwen carry serving dishes to the table and then had left the room. I'd wanted to get a chance to speak to her before we left, but was afraid I'd have to try to catch her in the kitchen.

Theo sat next to me, hunched over, moving the food around on his plate. I didn't see Frenchie's carrier so I wondered if he'd left the pup in his room. If he'd raise his head and make eye contact, I would ask him.

I glanced across the table at Dixie, who was in a discussion with Gwen about some of the recipes. J.J. and Jezzie were having a conversation about a planned business expansion. Jezzie was for it, J.J. was not—or at least that's what I gathered. The more wine Jezzie had, the louder her voice got, so in short order I'd have more details.

I reached for my knife and accidentally bumped Theo's arm. He looked up.

"Sorry," I apologized.

"No problem," he answered. "I'm afraid I've not been very good company."

"It's understandable." I cut through the tender prime rib. "It's a tough time."

"Mmm." He finally took a bite of the food he'd been moving around.

"No word from the sheriff?" I asked.

"No. Hopefully tomorrow he can get in touch with someone from Colette's work."

"Are you involved with the family business?" I'd assumed he was, but since we'd been at Arbor House it didn't seem that any of the business discussions involved him. Only J.J. and Jezzie.

"Not really." He shook his head. "Mother would like to see me more involved, but…" He shrugged.

"From what I understand, business is good."

"It is." Theo gave me a sharp look and I wondered what that was about. My comment had been sort of a generic throwaway remark. The kind of thing you say when you really don't know anything about the topic.

Finding that subject a dead end, I tried again.

"I've never done archery. Are you an archer like the rest of the family?" The minute the question was out of my mouth, I felt my cheeks heat as I realized how insensitive it was.

Luckily, Theo didn't take offense.

"Not as good as the rest, no," he responded. "My mother and uncles have been into archery since they were kids. Mostly taught by my grandmother."

"Your grandmother?" I was surprised. "I would have thought your grandfather."

"No, Grand-mère is the champion in the family. When I was little they used to go on hunting expeditions to Canada."

"What?" I couldn't picture it. "What would they hunt?"

"Deer, elk, wild turkey," he answered. "I even remember one time when they went on a bear hunt."

"That's amazing." More than amazing. I was blown away. And it meant any one of them had the skill to have killed Colette.

"That right. With Grand-mère leading the way." Theo smiled. "She's quite the lady and tougher than she looks."

There was a clatter that interrupted conversation as Jezzie dropped her fork onto her plate. "Well, this is a fine time to suddenly take an interest." She spoke to her brother, but her voice carried down the length of the table.

J.J. pushed back his chair and started to respond, but was interrupted by Jonathan.

"Could we leave this until after dinner?" he asked.

There was a look between the two brothers and then J.J. pulled his chair back up to the table. Jezzie looked from one to the other and took a drink of her wine.

The family seemed so on edge that I wasn't sorry we were leaving right after dinner. Dixie and I offered to help clear the table, but Gwen insisted they were fine.

My guess was after the stress of what they'd been through they were ready to have the house to themselves.

And who could blame them.

A death that may or may not be accidental in the middle of what was supposed to be a fun family get-together.

Memorable. But not your warm and fuzzy memories-to-cherish kind of family reunion.

* * * *

As we finished packing up and left Arbor House Sunday evening, Friday night's dinner seemed a lifetime away. My idealistic view of family and relationships had been called into question more than once. And Dixie and I were more than ready to head home.

The house was still beautiful, but maybe a little less fairy-like in my eyes. The sunset washed the sky in shades of pink, lighting the house and creating shadows.

I felt my eyes drawn to the corner of the house where I'd seen someone the past two nights. And I now knew, it hadn't just been my imagination.

Gwen and Jonathan were the only ones who came to see us off. The rest of the family had gone back to their solitary pursuits.

We climbed in the Jeep and waved good-bye. Setting the GPS for home, I turned onto the roadway. We hadn't gone far when my phone bleeped with a text message.

I handed it to Dixie. "Would you take a look?"

She read it and smiled. "It's Max and he wants to know how things went."

"Tell him, *it's a long story* and then do one of those smiley faces that isn't smiling but isn't frowning."

"You mean this one." She showed me one with hearts for eyes.

"No." I shook my head.

"How about this one?" Holding the phone so I could see, she'd picked the one with crazy eyes.

"That's probably the most relevant one, but not what I had in mind." I stayed focused on the road, listening carefully for my prompts from Matilda, my GPS lady. I did not want to get lost.

"Okay, I'll stop messing with you." She made a few keystrokes and hit the button. "There—it's sent."

"Thanks."

"How are things going with Max, by the way?"

"Really great." I smiled. "Once we relaxed and stopped trying to figure out what our relationship was, we—"

"Turn left in one-half mile," my GPS interrupted.

"Thanks, Matilda," I said before continuing.

Dixie shook her head.

I ignored her.

"We both got over ourselves," I continued my previous answer. "And things got a lot better. We're taking it slow."

"I'm glad you're figuring things out." Dixie handed me back my phone.

"I'm not saying I don't still get all worried and insecure if I don't hear from him. And I probably drive him crazy with wanting to know everything he's doing, every thought he's thinking," I explained.

"I'm sure." Dixie nodded.

"Hey, what do you mean by that?" I asked. "We're working on getting to know each other better and that's a good place for both of us right now."

"You know the whole town thinks differently, don't you?" She shifted to face me.

"What do you mean?" I glanced over at her.

"It goes something like this… You and Max were seen at dinner, and last Saturday you two were also spotted at Travers Jewelry. According to the St. Ignatius grapevine, that is."

"Hell's bells, Dixie," I huffed. "We did go to dinner, but we were at the jewelry store because Max needed to replace the battery in his watch. It's a really nice one and he didn't want to scratch the back trying to do it himself."

I turned my head to glare at her.

"Hey, eyes on the road and please don't shoot the messenger. I'm only telling you what the gossip is that's going around."

"I'm done talking about Max and me." I couldn't believe what people inferred from what they'd seen. "Let's talk about murder instead."

We spent the remaining miles, occasionally interrupted by Matilda giving directions, discussing what we knew and didn't know about Colette. And what possible motives there could be to kill her.

That was, of course, if it didn't end up being an accident.

Chapter Eight

Monday morning Dixie was in the kitchen area of Sugar and Spice Cookbooks, putting the final touches on some cupcakes and I was in the office putting the final touches on some bills, when the chime at the front entrance dinged.

My guess was Disco, a fellow business owner with a memorabilia shop called Flashback that was located a few doors down. You might wonder at the name.

Not the shop, but his name. I mean, naming your kid Disco is right up there with naming your kid Apple, or Moon Unit or North.

This guy, however, wasn't really named Disco. He had a real name, but I often forgot what it was because everyone in town called him Disco. His store had struggled for a while but he'd made a move into internet sales and seemed to be doing better. But not so much better that he'd stopped coming by our shop to see what Dixie had been cooking. And if there might be samples.

Can't blame him. Dixie's baking is always amazing.

I stuck my head out of my office to make sure it was him.

Our morning visitor was not Disco this time. It was none other than Sheriff Griffin. I set the bills aside and went out front.

"Hi, Terry." I know it sounds overly familiar, but he'd given me permission to use his first name a couple of dead bodies ago. I'd easily adjusted to using it when he was out of uniform, but I had a more difficult time with the first-name basis when he had his here-in-an-official-capacity duds on.

Like today.

"Good morning." He nodded briefly.

Terry was good-looking in a high-school jock that had aged well sort of way. No chemistry there for me other than in a friend sense, but if he and Dixie were in the same room the chemistry was on the Bananas Foster flaming-alert scale.

"Hey." Dixie walked out from the back with a tray laden with lemon blueberry cupcakes and held it out to him.

Terry looked at her, looked at the cupcakes, smiled, and picked one up.

They paused, time stopped, birds sang. Like I was saying.

"What's new in the Arbor family case?" I asked, hating to break the spell, but was unable to tamp down my curiosity, even in the name of love.

"Quite a bit." Terry took his cupcake, shifted his duty belt, and sat on the edge of one of the stools at the polished counter that took up most of the space in our main area.

Dixie and I joined him.

"Like what?" Dixie asked, sliding the tray onto the polished quartz countertop.

He paused to lick a bit of frosting from his thumb and we almost lost Dixie again. She leaned forward, watching intently.

I kicked her shin.

"Ouch." She frowned at me.

I raised my brows, sending her pay-attention vibes, but she ignored me.

"Well, for one, the tip that was on the arrow that killed Colette was a hunting arrowhead." He set down his cupcake, his fingers now sticky from the frosting.

"What does that mean in terms of who shot the arrow?" I asked.

"The target-practice arrowheads are entirely different." He looked around and Dixie handed him a paper napkin from under the counter.

"So, it could be hunters, then?" I asked.

"Could be." He was a man of few words.

"Or someone who intended to kill her," Dixie finished for him.

"What about the cigarette butt?" I asked.

Sheriff Terry rubbed his chin. "I questioned all the family members. Not a smoker among them. They gave me names of people who work on the property. I'll start with them next."

"Sorry," I sighed. "I thought it might be a good lead."

"It still may be." He stood. "Are you two headed back there anytime soon?"

Ah. The real reason for his visit. Except for Dixie, of course.

"Max and I are heading to Arbor House tomorrow afternoon to get some formal photos of the family for the book." I reached for one of the cupcakes for myself.

Dixie eyed me but to her credit she didn't say anything. Her cupcakes and cookies—and scones and biscuits—were the whole reason I'd had to take my walking to the next level. Since going into business with her, I'd already gained ten pounds and was well on my way to fifteen if I didn't get things under control.

The thing was, I loved food. Which meant I was more than willing to do whatever I needed to do, whether it was three thousand extra steps, five thousand extra steps—whatever—in order to have one of those cupcakes.

I checked my wrist. Already at 7,312 for the day. I'd been out for an early-morning walk before I left home. I figured I'd only need to add a couple of thousand more to offset the cupcake.

Okay, the truth is I have no idea how many steps it would take to earn a lemon blueberry cupcake. I would have to ask my friend Google when I got the chance.

Dixie and Terry stared at me and I realized I hadn't exactly been paying attention.

"Sorry. What was that?"

"Terry asked what time you're going." Dixie smirked.

"Max is picking me up tomorrow after lunch." I gave her a glare and took a big bite of the cupcake.

The bell dinged again and this time it actually was Disco. Like a guided missile homing in on a target, he came in the front door and headed directly for the tray of cupcakes.

"Wow, man." Holding back his shoulder-length hair and looking over his wire-rimmed glasses, he leaned in for a closer look. "What are those?"

"Cupcakes." I wondered what he meant. I knew he'd seen cupcakes before.

"Whoa, but they're blue, dude."

The only dude in the room was Sheriff Terry, but for Disco "dude" was a generic term.

"Blueberries," Dude Dixie answered. "Try one if you like."

Disco whipped out a tie-dyed kerchief and carefully placed two of the cupcakes in the middle.

The sheriff's phone rang and he quickly answered. "This is Sheriff Griffin."

Disco took advantage of our preoccupation with attempting to eavesdrop on the sheriff's phone call to skedaddle out of there.

"See you later, alligators," he called as he tromped off, cradling his summer of love cupcakes carrier.

"See you later," I responded before turning back into the sheriff and his call.

"Thank you." He tapped the phone to end the call and slipped it in his pocket. He waited a full minute, watching our expectant faces.

I couldn't take it any longer.

"Sheriff, put us out of our misery," I begged.

"We contacted the firm where the young woman was employed and they supplied her emergency contacts."

"And?" Dixie prompted.

"And they're all fake." He wiped a hand over his face. "Every last one of them."

"Fake?" I couldn't believe it. "Who does that?"

"Fake," he confirmed. "Phony names, addresses, phone numbers."

"I guess that means you're back to square one, right?" Dixie asked.

"Exactly." The sheriff paused. "I have a dead girl, but no next of kin to contact. I have what may or may not be an accidental death. Hunting season, but no hunters spotted in the area. And I have a family of archers, but no one, as far as we can tell, with any reason to want the dead girl dead."

"Wow, talk about a dead end."

Dixie and the sheriff both gave me a hard look.

"When you and Max are there tomorrow, I'd appreciate it if you'd keep your eyes and ears open."

"I can do that." I nodded, thinking the request almost made me a deputy. Not a real deputy, you understand, but like a citizen deputy.

"Do you think it's okay for Sugar to go?" Dixie asked. "Do you think she's in any danger?"

"No, I don't believe she is." Terry shook his head. "But Sugar, remember: I'm only asking you to keep your eyes and ears open. No snooping, no digging, no asking questions."

"Got it." I sighed. Okay, maybe not so much like a citizen deputy. Still, it would kind of be like I was working undercover, right? I liked that idea.

The sheriff left and Dixie and I got back to what we'd been working on. I had returned to working on the bills when I heard the front door ding again.

"Hey, dudes." Our retro friend was back and this time the tie-dyed kerchief was tied across his forehead like a headband.

"Hey, Disco." I left my desk and headed out front again. "You haven't eaten both of those cupcakes already, have you?"

"Actually, yeah, I did." He looked sheepish. "But that's not why I'm here. I forgot to tell you what I came to tell you earlier."

"What was that?"

"I forgot to ask whether you were going to the Square Merchants meeting."

Now, Disco didn't mean that we were "square" in the dull and uninteresting sense of the word, nor as in a hip-to-be-square sort of reference. Though some of us might qualify for that description. He meant the association for the businesses located around the town square.

There were probably twenty to twenty-five businesses around the outside of the streets that faced a lush green space with the historic limestone Jameson County Courthouse at its center.

Merchants meetings were held quarterly unless something in particular was going on. We'd had a special meeting in the summer about getting together to have flower baskets attached to the light poles.

They turned out really pretty and now that the summer pansies were fading out, there had been some interest in filling the baskets with fall flowers. I couldn't imagine Disco had a great interest in that topic. However, there was always food at these meetings.

"About flowers?" I asked.

"Nah, it's about Glue Man."

"Who?" I was taken aback.

Was Glue Man some new superhero?

Look out Superman, Spiderman, and Aquaman. There's a new man in town. Glue Man.

Or maybe a new breed of vandal. We'd had a problem a while back with graffiti. Maybe this prankster glued things down so you couldn't move them. Imagine your glass glued down at a restaurant or your lawn chairs glued to your porch or maybe even your mailbox glued shut. The possibilities were endless.

"You know." Disco glanced around. I wasn't sure if he was looking out for Glue Man or checking to see if Dixie had more cupcakes. "He's the guy that invented that glue that is so strong you can glue a guy to a steel beam. Though why you'd want to glue a guy, I dunno."

I'm afraid I'd missed that. I was unaware of Glue Man and his super-duper glue.

"Why are we meeting about him?"

"Cuz he wants to open up a store on the square, but Harry thinks it will hurt his business."

Harry had Harrison's Hardware store on the opposite side of the square from us. He'd managed it for years and had recently bought it lock, stock, and barrel from the Farmer family. It was an institution in town and carried everything from paper clips to power tools.

"I don't see how. But in any case, you can't keep out competition."

"That's what Toy George said. Said she didn't fuss when that submarine sandwich place opened last year."

"Back to the meeting. When is it?" I asked.

"Tonight. In the back room at the Red Hen Diner," Disco explained. "I didn't know if you guys got the notice since you've been out of town."

"I didn't see it." We hadn't been very far out of town or gone very long, for that matter. But it was nice of Disco to think of us. "Thanks, Disco. I'll let Dixie know."

"Okay, groovy. Got to get back." He ambled out.

I wandered back to where Dixie was sorting through some more of the Arbor family recipe cards. There were a ton.

"Who was that?" she asked.

"That was Disco again. He was back because the real reason he'd stopped by earlier wasn't just for cupcakes. He wanted to tell us about the Square Merchants meeting tonight."

"About what?" She set the recipe cards aside.

"It's about Glue Man."

"Glue Man?" Dixie opened the notebook for the other project we were working on. "What does he have to do with us?"

"I suppose you know about Glue Man."

"Of course." Dixie grinned. "He's the guy with the glue so strong you can glue a man to a steel beam."

Whoa. How had I missed this exciting product?

"He's opening a store and some of the merchants, or at least one, Harry Harrison, doesn't think that's a good idea." I shared what Disco had told me.

"Unless there's something inherently wrong with his plans or his operation, we can't simply decide we don't want a particular store." Dixie shrugged her shoulders.

"That's what I said." I nodded. "And also, according to Disco, what Toy George said."

"Disco's planning to go to the meeting?" she asked.

"He is. But it might be partly for the free food. It's at the Red Hen Diner."

"We should probably go." She sighed. "If they're wound up about this, there may be a need for some level heads."

"Any group is in trouble if they're counting on us for level heads." I picked up a few of the recipe cards. "But I get your point."

* * * *

"Cluck." The chime at the front door of the Red Hen Diner announced us as we entered. A unique feature of the diner was the chicken theme and the door chime was your first clue. From there, rooster tiles lined the walls, the place mats had silhouettes of chickens; even the salt and pepper shakers were baby chicks. And don't even get me started on the menu.

The restaurant was packed with dinner patrons and the meeting room at the diner was almost full when we arrived. The tables were set up in a U-shape, with the food set up off to the side on a different table.

Don't tell Dixie, but, like Disco, part of what had convinced me to come was the promise of pie from Toy George's kitchen at the Red Hen.

I latched onto a plate with a slice of cherry pie as we passed the food table and none too soon, because it looked like it was the next-to-the-last piece. Now, I would've settled for apple or peach if I had to, but Toy's cherry pie had been on my mind ever since we'd decided to attend.

The chatter in the room sounded like less like a merchants business meeting and more like a gaggle of geese had congregated in the space.

Pouring myself a cup of coffee—because what's pie without coffee—I found a spot to sit down. Dixie, not as quick on the draw as me, had been left with fewer choices, but had managed to score a slice of lemon meringue.

She sat down next to me. "Looks like the gang's all here." She nodded toward the group.

Toy George was across the room chatting with Tina Martin from Jameson County Real Estate. Tina was also a beauty consultant with Looking Pretty Cosmetics, one of those companies where they have parties to convince you to buy the products. I hoped Tina wasn't talking Toy into having a Looking Pretty party, because that would result in Dixie and I getting roped in again. Dixie still hadn't forgiven me for the last time I had caved. She swore it had taken her days to get all the layers of makeup off her face.

Lark Travers, who owned the jewelry store next door to us, listened as a very animated Tressa, who had the hair salon the other direction from our shop, talked. Based on her hand gestures and facial expressions, Tressa must have had strong views about Glue Man and his planned store. Or maybe not. Come to think of it, Tressa was always very expressive, even if she was just talking to you about, say, your sandwich.

Glen Page, news reporter for the *St. Ignatius Journal*, was also on hand. The paper must think the discussion was newsworthy to send Glen instead of their young cub reporter.

"Shall we get started?" Krissie, who owned the bakery on the corner, and who must have been the current Square Merchants Association chair, stood and tapped her fork against her water glass to get everyone's attention. "If you'll all take your seats, please, we can begin." Krissie was a cute blonde with a soccer-mom look, a sugar-sweet voice, and a *Shark Tank* business mind.

Those who had been standing obligingly found a place to sit, and the room quieted.

"First off, I have a letter to read from the company, Glue Man Group."

I was the only one in the room who snickered.

Dixie gave me a "straighten-up" look.

Krissie read the letter, which was all about how the company hoped the St. Ignatius community would be welcoming. The glue was currently and would continue to be produced elsewhere. I'd wondered about that.

What they were looking for was a place to serve as an outlet where customers could get the glue directly, and a place where they could handle shipping.

Coming to the end of the letter, Krissie folded it, put it back in the envelope, and looked up. "Comments?"

"I don't see why Milo and Luella had to lease their space to this kind of a company," Harry protested. "There are tons of local folks who'd be happy to have that prime spot."

"I'm afraid they didn't get many offers," Lark Travers noted.

"Or at least none for that kind of money," Toy chimed in.

"They didn't give it time," Harry shot back. "They were in a big hurry to get to their place in Florida before the snow flies."

"Can you blame them?" Dixie commented under her breath.

The group went back and forth with a handful of actual concerns coming out in the discussion. Those were mostly around the volume of shipping and whether the location was equipped for that. You'd have to think a company that had already enjoyed some success had looked into that, right? But it was a fair question.

Most of the rest of the worries were around the changes that might occur as a result of having a different type of company on the square.

"Change is inevitable, though, and if we stop changing, we'll die," Dixie spoke up, "like so many small towns around the state. If you'll remember, when I first talked to you all about Sugar and Spice Cookbooks, you were reluctant. The location we're in had always been a food establishment: a doughnut shop, a bistro, a cake store. What we were proposing was different."

"That's true," Grace Nelson, the proprietor of a small shop that stocked locally made wine, agreed. "We weren't sure how a business that wasn't actually a store would fit in."

"I say we give them a chance to answer our questions." Dixie raised her voice to be heard over the din of side conversations that had started up again.

There were several nods of agreement.

Krissie jumped on the whiff of consensus. "Okay then, if we're all good with that as a next step, I'll write back with all of the questions you've asked. And we'll await a response from the Glue Man Group."

Dixie swiveled her head to look at me, but this time I suppressed the snicker.

"I think they probably need to talk to an attorney before they get into too much of a rush." I stabbed the last piece of pie with my fork and waved it toward the room in general. "My guess that if the zoning and all that allows it, there's very little that can be done."

"I'm sure you're right about that." Dixie finished the final bite of her pie as well, and stood. "Ready?"

"I am," I responded.

We had walked over from the office so I could get a few more steps in. We'd hoped the meeting would be short and it hadn't been too bad.

We dropped our plates and silverware in the tub that had been provided for dirty dishes and headed toward the door. But we found our path blocked by the St. Ignatius news reporter.

"Would you like to give a comment on the murder at Arbor House?" He used his big broadcast voice, like he was announcing a best-selling mystery novel.

How the news had traveled to St. Ignatius so quickly, I didn't know. I'm sure the local news had covered Colette's death, but there'd been no mention of us. And I knew the sheriff hadn't shared any information. They'd interviewed him on TV but he'd been terse in his responses.

I think it went something like, "I can't comment. The investigation is ongoing." Followed by "No comment" on all the follow-up questions from the television reporter from the local affiliate.

"Glen, they don't know that it's a murder." Dixie continued walking.

"That's right," I confirmed, "it's just a suspicious death." I too continued toward the door.

But it was too late.

The room had gone silent.

I slowly swiveled, but I could feel all the eyes on us before I turned.

"You girls are involved in a murder again?" Toy George asked from across the room. "You'd better get back in here and fill us in."

Chapter Nine

The following afternoon, Max pulled into my driveway right on time.

I smiled and waved at Mrs. Pickett, who was outside raking leaves in her housecoat. With curlers in her hair. Wearing yellow rain boots.

It was early autumn and very few leaves had fallen so far. But knowing Mrs. Pickett, no doubt she'd decided to tackle them early. She didn't wave back.

Max picking me up in his Land Rover would give her something to stew about for a while.

As we headed out of town, I asked Max if he needed any help with finding the bed-and-breakfast. He'd never been there and it wasn't the easiest to find. But he said he'd looked it up and thought he was good.

I'm pretty sure that was his polite way of saying he didn't trust my directions. He's a smart guy.

On the drive there we talked about how things were going with his photo projects and how unseasonably cool it had been. We chatted about what we were reading. Me, a new historical mystery by a new-to-me author. Him, a group biography of several photographers told by a former assistant to Ansel Adams. I shared the latest cat antics from my house and he shared his most recent homeowner/landowner woes. We talked about anything and everything.

That is, everything except the death at Arbor House. Which was fine by me after the grilling Dixie and I had been through after the Square Merchants meeting last night.

Max drove directly to the road where the bed-and-breakfast was located, and I pointed out the sign that marked the entrance.

When we made the turn into the drive, I waited for Max's reaction. The place was stunning. I'd likened it to a fairy house the first time I'd seen it and had hoped one day for both Dixie and Max to get the opportunity.

I watched as his photographer's gaze roved over the three-story Victorian, soft pastels of the paint, the vivid colors of the flowers and trees, and so unexpected here in the middle of nowhere.

He turned and smiled at me, a flash and a twinkle in his blue eyes. "I see why you like it so much."

* * * *

It was odd being back at Arbor House. The family had collected in the living room to be photographed.

Max was great with food photos and I'd also seen some of his outdoor work, which was his specialty, but I'd never actually seen him work with people. I'd given him an idea of the type of pictures we were looking to include in the cookbook, but I also knew he often had his own ideas. And truth be told, they were often better than mine.

The only instruction he'd asked me to give the family was that he'd like them to avoid patterns in their clothing. Solid colors. It seemed they'd all complied. Although they were mostly conservative dressers. In fact, come to think of it, I'd not seen any of them in much of anything with wild patterns.

I introduced Max to the group and then stood aside to let him do his thing.

Positioning the whole group on the stairs, he took several shots.

"What about the possibility of getting a few photos of you eating together?" he asked. "That would fit in well with what you're going for, wouldn't it, Sugar?"

I nodded. "It would."

"Lucinda had found some older photos of a family get-together I believe at this very table. I had thought I might include it." I stopped. "With your approval, of course." I looked across the room to the eldest, Joe, Jr.

"J.J., are you being difficult?" Lucinda asked. "It's not a top-secret photo and it's not unflattering to any of you. Surely you know I wouldn't do that."

"I'm sure he just wants to make sure the family is shown in the best light." Jezzie gave her a hard look. "What with this murder and everything."

She turned to look at Theo like she thought it was his fault for bringing Colette. How very inconvenient of her to get shot with an arrow.

Max turned to me again. "So you don't want a photo of them at the dining room table or you do?"

"It would be great to have a more current one to put with the vintage one if everyone is amenable to that," I answered.

"If there isn't time, can I come back and do that?" Max asked. "Is everyone here or are there more coming?"

"No, this is everyone. And it's silly to have you make another trip." Gwendolyn stood. "If it's convenient, why don't you and Sugar stay and have dinner with us. I know Sugar is dying to chat with Lucinda about her genealogy research because they didn't get to it during the weekend. And I'm sure one of us can show you around the property or find you a corner where you can put your feet up."

Max nodded in my direction. "That works for me, but it's up to Sugar."

"I can make that work." I waited. "If it's okay with all of you."

There were nods from all and so it was decided.

"I'd also like a group photo on the front porch, if you don't mind." Max broke the awkwardness. "The lighting is great this late in the day and the colors of the house and flowers will add some nice contrast."

"Come on, let's get moving so I can get a nap in before dinner." Marta hadn't spoken up until now.

I wondered what she thought of the tension between her children and their spouses. It was probably good there was a limit to this family reunion of sorts.

Everyone filed out to the porch. Max seated Marta in a white wicker chair and let the others position themselves around her. Jonathan and Gwen stood beside the chair, arms around each other. J.J., the tallest, was directly behind his mother with Lucinda beside him, and then Jezzie and Tom on the other side. It was a nice family photo.

Max moved a few of the flowerpots to get the effect he wanted and then asked if everyone was ready.

"Wait." Jezzie looked around. "Where's Theo?"

Had he not come outside when we all filed out?

"I'm right here." He spoke from the doorway, where he stood with a glass of wine in his hand. "Don't have a cow, Mother."

"You can't blame me for being nervous, with the way things have gone since we arrived," she snapped.

"Where do you want me?" he asked Max, draining his wine and setting the glass on a small table.

"Let's try something." Max pointed. "Would you sit near your grandmother's feet?"

"No problem." Theo positioned himself on the porch floor at Marta's feet.

It really was a great grouping: The family, all beautiful in their own way, the muted colors they wore, the riot of flowers, and the soft tones of the siding as a backdrop. Max took a lot of shots. I knew from experience he'd sort them out later and select a few of the best ones for Dixie and me to look at. Or in this case, for the family.

"Thanks, everyone." He was finally done and the group began to disperse. Walking over to where I stood leaning against the porch railing, he stopped. "Was it really okay with you for us to stick around until mealtime?"

"Absolutely." I brushed off my skirt. "Gwen was correct. I have been wanting to spend some time with Lucinda but haven't had a chance. If she's free, I'll take her up on her offer to show me how she's been doing her research."

"Still wanting to find your father's family?" he asked.

"I am." I nodded. "I've always wanted to, but the box of his things has made me even more curious." A few months back I'd gotten a package from my father's agent. A few photos, some personal effects, and an unfinished manuscript. There had been very few clues, but from what Lucinda had shared with me, it sounded like even a few clues gave you a place to start.

"Can you keep yourself busy?" I asked.

"Plenty to photograph." He glanced around. "I'll check and make sure of where I can and can't go."

"You'd probably better check with J.J.," I noted. "He seems to be the one who is particular about what's fair game and what's not."

"Yeah, I noticed that." He looped his camera bag over his shoulder and headed toward the door. Holding it open, he motioned me ahead. "After you."

Lucinda stood chatting with Jonathan, who had his computer out. She looked up as we came inside.

"Would you like to see what I'm doing?" she asked.

"I would," I responded.

"Follow me." She motioned toward the stairs. "The downstairs study is for guests, but upstairs there's another. It must have been another library of sorts, and I've been using it for my work area while I'm here."

"Anything I can help you with?" Jonathan addressed Max. While his tone was polite, I detected a bit of relief when Max shook his head.

"No, I'm good." He tapped his camera. "I'd like to look around the property a bit, if that's okay."

"No problem." Jonathan went back to whatever he'd been doing on his computer.

"Sugar seemed to think I should check with your brother, J.J.," Max clarified. "Do I need to do that?"

"I think the only area you need to avoid is where the police have marked it off with that yellow plastic," Jonathan answered. "But J.J. is out back if you want to check."

"Got it," Max responded and headed outside.

I turned and followed Lucinda to the stairs.

"Seems like maybe you and our photographer are more than business associates," Lucinda noted as we made our way up the staircase.

"We're friends as well." Not sure how much I wanted to share about my relationship with Max, I gave her the simplest answer.

"He looks at you like it's more than friends."

I felt my cheeks warm. I liked that idea, but like I'd told Dixie, we were taking things slow.

Lucinda opened the first door at the top of the stairs to a book-lined room. There was a very large table in the middle of the room and a rolltop desk off to the side. The table was covered with files and an open laptop sat on one side.

"Wow." I took in the stacks of papers, photographs, and newspaper clippings. "You've been busy." I was glad for the change in topic.

"I have, but I enjoy the research." She laid a hand on the computer. "I did it in dribs and drabs when I was still working, but now that I have the time, I'm able to dig a little deeper."

"What did you do before you retired?" I hadn't thought to ask before.

"I was a history teacher."

No wonder she was so interested in family history.

"I've been digging into my family's background for quite a while and my family is from this county as well. So, when I came across records that related to the Arbor family, I've been saving those. It's amazing how many times our families crossed paths."

"I have to confess that I have no idea where to start," I told her. "You may regret offering to show me the ropes, because I am a complete beginner."

"Don't worry about that." She lifted some files off one of the chairs. "Have a seat and I'll show you some basics."

I settled into the chair and she handed me a yellow pad.

"First off, write down everything you know."

"I'm afraid it's not very much at all."

"That's okay." She tapped the tablet. "Write it down and we'll start from there."

I did as she asked.

"Okay, let's start with getting you familiar with some of the tools at your disposal." She pulled the computer toward us.

We spent the next hour and a half with Lucinda showing me places where I could begin looking for records related to my father's adoptive parents. I was amazed at the number of free resources that were available. I filled a page with notes on websites with access to public records.

"You should teach a class for people who are, like me, starting down this path."

"I may at some point, but right now, I'm trying to spend my time putting together as much as I can of the Brevard family. Hopefully, I can leave my daughter with more knowledge of her ancestors than I had."

"Oh, I'm sorry, I didn't realize that you and J.J. had a daughter." I'd been under the impression that Theo was the only grandchild.

"We don't. My daughter is from my first marriage," she explained. "Calle is the only good thing that came of it."

"Does she live close by?" I asked. "Will she be joining you for the week here?"

"She's away at college, I'm afraid." Lucinda tucked a lock of salt-and-pepper hair behind her ear. "It's taken her a while, but she's finishing up a doctorate in women's history."

"Have you and J.J. been married long, then?" I realized as soon as the words were out of my mouth how nosy the question sounded. "I'm sorry, that's none of my business."

"No problem." She laughed. "We met at college. Not when we were attending college like normal people, but much later. I was teaching a history class and J.J. was auditing the class. I suppose we might have come across each other as children because my family came from this area, but I don't remember him at all.

"My family was poor; my father died when I was young, my mother raised me and my sister all on her own. I'm not sure what happened with my father, but there were a lot of secrets around the house. That's probably what drove me to research the past." She leaned back from the computer with a wistful look in her eyes.

"Not dissimilar to my family, except that my father and mother divorced, and with Daddy not around and him being a topic my mother was reluctant to discuss, I have very little background to go on. As you can see." I pointed at the paper.

"Well, I think we have a place for you to start." Lucinda set aside the papers she'd been showing me and stood. "I don't know about you, but I could use something cold to drink."

"Sounds good to me." I stood also and stretched my legs. My step-tracker reminded me that I had a long way to go to meet my goal for the day. The car ride had not helped at all and then I'd sat talking with Lucinda for the past hour or so.

We made our way down the stairs and into the living room, which was deserted. Hearing voices from the direction of the kitchen, we followed the sounds.

Max leaned against the center island. He wore a bright orange vest over his clothes.

"We definitely can see you coming," I noted.

"J.J. suggested I put this on because I wanted to go into the woods, and since it is hunting season it would make me easy to spot."

Given that Colette had been wearing a dark green jacket when I found her, it seemed like a good idea. I kept thinking if it turned out to be a hunting accident, it could be that coat had worked against her. If she'd worn the bright pink coat she'd had on when she arrived, the outcome might have been different.

Maybe the hunters would have seen her.

Maybe it would have saved her life.

In any case, I was glad that control-freak J.J. had insisted on a neon orange vest for Max.

It took me a few minutes, but I realized there was someone else in the kitchen and she was also wearing a bright orange vest.

"Sugar, this is Libby." Max swept his hand toward the girl. "Libby, this is Sugar Calloway and Lucinda Arbor."

"Nice to meet you." The girl had a slight accent that I couldn't place.

"I came across Libby in the woods." Max took a swig from the water bottle he'd just filled. "A fellow photographer."

She was tall and slender with a bit of a muscular build. I could imagine her tromping around the woods. Her jeans and light flannel shirt looked like she'd been prepared for hiking. That's not to say she wasn't feminine. She wore small gold hoop earrings and a half-heart necklace. You know, one of those where someone else wore the other half. I thought her to be about thirty.

I'm terrible at guessing ages, so I could have been way off. Let's just say she was somewhere between sixteen and sixty.

"I didn't realize I was trespassing." Libby pushed dark blond hair out of her face. "But Max introduced me to your family," she said, smiling at Lucinda, "and got me cleared for picture-taking."

She held up a camera that looked expensive but not quite as fancy as Max's. I didn't know a lot about photography equipment, but I was learning. My photo skills were limited to adorable pictures of Ernest, my very photogenic cat, when he was sleeping and pictures I accidentally took of my feet when I didn't realize I had the camera app open.

"Are you staying nearby?" Lucinda asked.

"I'm staying in…uhm…Doorsville?" She hesitated.

"Dewersville," Lucinda corrected. "It's a nice little town. Post office, motel, convenience store. No restaurant."

"That's the place." Libby nodded.

"Maybe you'd like to join us for dinner," Lucinda added.

Maybe she should check with J.J. and Jezzie, I thought. Though the house now belonged to Jonathan and Gwen, it seemed like the older brother had taken over deciding who should do what with the family in residence.

"Oh, I couldn't impose," the girl protested.

"It's no trouble at all to set another place, is it?" Lucinda turned to Gwen, who had just entered the kitchen.

Gwen held out her hand. "Hi, I'm Gwendolyn Arbor."

"I'm Libby." Long, slim fingers that had been fiddling with her camera took Gwen's hand. "I couldn't interrupt your family festivities."

"Well, they've already been interrupted." Jezzie had joined the group. "Who are you?"

"Jezz, this is Libby," Gwen explained. "She's going to be joining us for dinner."

"But—" Libby started to say something.

"No buts, I insist." Gwen held up a hand. "Now, I also insist that you all get out of this kitchen and let Hilda and me work or nobody's going to be having dinner." She waved us all out the door.

"I've got drinks and appetizers set out on the sideboard in the dining room. You know where the glasses are, so help yourselves."

"How long?" Jezzie asked.

"The casseroles are premade and have already thawed, so thirty to forty minutes." Gwen answered. "Now, shoo. All of you."

"Thank you for inviting me." Libby fell into step with Lucinda. "Is there somewhere I could wash up?"

"Sure." Lucinda touched the girl's arm. "Follow me."

The rest of us filed into the dining room where there was a large spread of summer veggies along with various dips.

Jonathan had assumed the role of host and offered drinks. I accepted a glass of wine, wishing for a chance to "wash up" myself. As soon as Lucinda returned, I would find out which bath they wanted us to use.

Lucinda had returned, but not Libby.

I made my way in her direction, but she was deep in conversation with Max about ruins.

Waiting for a chance to interrupt, I couldn't seem to find a break. It seemed the Mayan ruins were endlessly fascinating to them both. And Lucinda hoped to return one day.

I would be in ruins myself if I didn't find a washroom soon. Looking around to see if Libby was back and maybe I could find out from her which way to go, I noticed Jezzie standing at the foot of the stairs.

"Is there a washroom I can use?" I asked.

"Top of the stairs." She took a big gulp of her wine and gestured toward the staircase with the glass.

"Thanks." I started up the stairs toward the second floor and as I reached the top step, I heard a door shut.

Libby stood in the hallway, shoving something into the pocket of her jeans. She looked startled to see me.

"I'm looking for the bathroom," I explained.

She pointed toward a partially open door on the left.

"Thanks. I'll see you downstairs, then." It couldn't have been the bathroom door I'd heard shut because that door was still open. Had she been down the hall snooping in some of the bedrooms? And if so, why? And what had she tucked away in her pocket so quickly?

I turned to ask her, but she was gone, already halfway down the stairs.

Arbor House had quite a few valuables and with the family in residence there were probably more. I hoped their welcoming spirit hadn't backfired on them. They'd been quick to include her but the truth was no one, Max included, knew much of anything about her.

Finishing my business quickly, I washed up and hurried back to the group.

I was sorry Dixie wasn't along to enjoy the dinner. Gwen had said the casseroles were premade but they sure didn't taste like it. With everyone's permission, Max took a few photos during dinner and then set his camera aside.

He was seated next to Libby and they discussed the merits of different cameras and digital editing suites. Sitting between Theo and Gwendolyn, I tried to listen in to see if Libby shared anything more about why she was in the area.

"What other projects are you working on?" Gwen touched my arm.

Her expression told me she'd probably asked more than once.

"We have a couple of other projects that are in the works. One is a little farther afield than we've gone to date. It's a Mississippi River town and they've collected recipes for dishes served on the steamboats of the past. Obviously, some influence from New Orleans, where many of the cruises ended up."

"That sounds like a great project with lots of great recipes to curate," she noted. "If you think about it, it's not unlike running a bed-and-breakfast. You're really catering to the clientele."

That's right." I nodded. "And there's also great history on the whole experience that we get the opportunity to sprinkle in."

"Like gambling history?" She took a sip of wine.

"That and more."

"Like what?" Lucinda asked from across the table.

"Well, some jazz history and also how steamboats function, and the life of a steamboat captain," I explained. "Maybe you were more aware, but I had no idea."

During our conversation, Theo had sat silently, moving food around on his plate, but eating little.

"How are things going with Frenchie?" I asked.

"What?" He looked up. Clearly his thoughts had been somewhere else. Understandable, I guess, given it had only been a few days since his fiancée was killed.

"The poodle?" I prompted.

"Oh, jeez. Not good." He wiped a hand over his face. "She doesn't like me. Won't mind. She's chewed up two pairs of my shoes. Italian leather."

Like it mattered what shoes. The poor little thing was stressed. I resisted saying the dog had good taste.

"Oh, no. Bless your heart." I patted his arm.

Southern training saved me again. It's okay to say it in your head, just not out loud. And if you need to slip in a "bless your heart" to keep from slapping the person silly. Well.

"She tolerated me with Colette around, but with Colette gone she's not adjusting well." He sighed. "But then, neither am I."

Okay, now I felt bad about wanting to slap him. "If there's anything I can do to help, just let me know."

"Thanks." He gave a slight smile. "I appreciate that."

"Any word on her family?" Even though I knew about the fake contacts from Sheriff Terry, I wanted to see if Theo would offer up the info.

"None," he mumbled.

"How much longer is the whole family staying?" I turned to Gwen.

"I'd initially blocked off these two weeks for the family." She took a sip of wine. "But with the events of the past few days, we're not sure of everyone's plans."

Once dinner was over, we carried our dishes to the kitchen.

Gwen was rinsing and handing them to Jonathan, who stacked them neatly in the dishwasher.

"No Hilda?" I asked.

"No." Gwen shook her head. "I sent Hilda on home tonight; these longer hours aren't what she signed up for. She usually just bakes and helps out in the kitchen. I have regular serving helpers, but I gave them time off these two weeks the family is here."

"You're lucky to have Hilda." I thought about Toy George and the trouble she had keeping waitresses at the Red Hen Diner. "It can be hard to find good workers."

"That's so true." Gwen rinsed another plate and handed it off. "We just get servers trained and then they go off to college. In the summer I have better luck, but this time of year, I'm working on finding replacements because my summer kids have left."

"Is there anything I can do to help with the dishes?" I felt guilty standing around talking while they were working.

"Would you want to take the coffee and tea out to the living room?" Gwen asked. "We'll be there in just a few minutes. I just like to get these started rather than have to face dishes later in the evening."

"Sure, no problem." I picked up the two carafes and headed back through the door.

In the living room everyone had settled into their seat of choice. Isn't it funny how we're all creatures of habit?

Jezzie in the leather tufted Queen Anne chair and J.J. in his spot by the fireplace. It wasn't cool enough for a fire, but I'd bet that was a cozy spot on a winter evening. Lucinda had once again claimed the chair by the table lamp and had her notebook out, flipping through pages.

Tom was as far as he possibly could get from the rest of the group and already had his phone out. His cheeks were ruddy and I don't think it was from being outside in the sunshine unless he'd found some way to practice his golf game.

Max and Libby were talking near the big picture window.

"Here's coffee and tea." I set the two containers on the table. Cups had already been arranged on a pretty tray in anticipation.

Theo touched my arm. "Grand-mère has gone up to her room, but says she owes you a chat. If you don't mind doing it now, she's available."

I hesitated, trying to catch Max's eye. I wasn't sure how much patience the older woman would have at the end of the day, but I'd take what time I could get.

Max wouldn't leave without me, right?

I followed Theo upstairs. I hadn't seen any of the family quarters during the time Dixie and I had been at Arbor House. Gwen had put her mother-in-law in what had to be the premier suite. It was at the back of the second floor and the sitting area had an expansive view of the woods behind the property. And, I imagined, of the archery range if you looked hard enough.

The furnishings, like the room we'd stayed in, were lush and yet homey. The king bed was heaped with soft pillows and the room was big enough to accommodate a deep burgundy velvet love seat that faced the fireplace.

"Thank you for seeing me, Mrs. Arbor."

She shifted the soft caramel-colored wrap on her narrow shoulders and motioned me in.

"Marta's fine." She was a woman of few words. I only hoped she had more to say as we talked and hadn't brought me here only to give me cryptic one-word answers.

"Shall we sit here?" I asked. The two chairs in the sitting area looked like the easiest spot to sit and talk.

"Yes, fine." She hobbled across the room.

"Do you need help?" I'd assumed she was more mobile since Theo had simply dropped me off at the door. But it looked like her ankle might be wrapped in a bandage.

"I do not." She seated herself in one chair and pointed for me to sit in the other. "Now, what is it you want to know about? I thought you and your friend were putting together a bunch of recipes in a book."

"That's the basic idea." I tried not to smile at her oversimplification. "But we also thought we'd include some stories with the recipes. Things like if there were times in particular when they were used. Celebrations, family gatherings, and that kind of thing."

"I see." Her dark eyes watched my face. "You have some you want to ask about?"

"Yes, I do." I'd pulled together ten recipes we were considering using as highlights. I handed the sheaf of papers to her. "Are there any of these that spark a memory or that you remember where you got the recipe?"

She flipped through each one and stopped on the quiche. "Ah, Quiche Me, the famous quiche that started it all."

"It must have been a struggle in the beginning," I prompted.

"It was hard work but fun. Lots of late nights preparing. Lots of early-morning rising at dawn, baking. We started with a small storefront and then as it got more popular, people were buying several and freezing them. And then Joe thinks, why don't we freeze them for the customers..."

"How did you go from that to a factory?" I tried to imagine that transition.

"That took money and we didn't have money." She patted her pocket and I wondered if she maybe needed a tissue or had a cell phone tucked away that had buzzed her. But she continued. "Joe borrowed money to get the start-up funds."

"Were you okay with that?"

"Didn't matter whether I was or not. I didn't have a say. Keep the house, keep the kids clean and quiet. Joe was very old-fashioned."

"Would he have approved of his daughter running the company?"

She was silent for a while and I figured I'd crossed the line with my last question.

She tucked the soft wrap around her and continued. "Jezzie was the only one interested. She was always in his office, at the factory, his constant shadow. When he died she was the one who knew the business inside and out."

"So, he left it to her."

"Oh, no. Joe thought he'd live forever. No life insurance. No will."

I wasn't sure how to ask the next question. Or if there was a way I could phrase it so it didn't seem so snoopy. Ah, well, sometimes you have to jump in and sink or swim.

"So then, who owns Arbor Family Foods?"

"We all do, but they want me to turn over my percentage. Or Jezzie does. Like I'm already dead." She reached for her side again. "She's ready to get bigger."

I heard the crackle in her pocket and saw the corner of a package and was struck dumb. "Wha—wha—what are you going to do?"

Good grief. Had I just seen what I thought I'd seen?

Could it have been Marta was outside both times? The shadowy figure by the house. The cigarette butts. It had been her. The pretender. I'd be willing to bet that was how she'd injured her ankle too.

She shrugged. "She wants to expand. Like my Joe, she'll figure out a way no matter how many arms she has to twist."

"Any memories on the other recipes?" I stepped to her chair and leaned in to point at one, taking a deep breath in the process. Oh, yeah, there it was. I could smell the cigarette smoke in her hair.

She looked up at me, her eyes cut to mine.

"It was you outside, wasn't it?" I asked.

"I don't know what you're talking about."

"Yes, you do, Marta." I wasn't backing down. "Both nights when I saw someone outside, it was you. I mentioned it to the sheriff and he talked to each one of you, but you didn't fess up."

"They all think I quit years ago. And I probably should have." She pulled the cigarette pack from her pocket. "Why should I tell on myself when it didn't really matter."

"But it did matter. The sheriff spent time on trying to figure out who'd been there."

"You want to talk recipes or not?"

"Fine." I went back and sat down.

We went on to talk about the recipes and as I suspected, there were some anecdotes and little tidbits around quite a few of the selections. A recipe that had been given to her by her mother on her wedding day. A secret ingredient in one of the pies that wasn't written down on the recipe card. A recipe for potato salad that was her own version of one she'd seen in a ladies' magazine and cut out, and then improved upon.

I jotted notes as we talked.

When I got up to leave, I thanked her for our time together and I truly meant it. These were just the type of tidbits that made a family cookbook so much more interesting.

As I started to leave, she stopped me.

"Wait."

"Yes." I turned to look at her.

"You're not going to bust me on the smoking, are you?"

"Marta, I have to tell the sheriff."

She sighed and sank back into her chair.

"I don't know that there's any reason for him to share it with your kids. But…" I gave her a stern look. "…you really do need to quit."

"So few vices left for old ladies." She frowned at me.

I let myself out and made my way downstairs.

Max gave me what I interpreted to be a where-have-you-been look. He was clearly ready to go and I was more than ready myself.

After a bit more polite after-dinner chat, Max and I thanked our hosts and took our leave. I especially thanked Lucinda for getting me started with my family research and promised to keep her apprised of my progress.

We were on our way to the Land Rover when I heard my name called. I turned back.

"Hey, Sugar." It was Theo who awkwardly held a squirming Frenchie. He caught up with us.

"Yes?"

"I know it's a huge imposition, but after we were talking at dinner, I was thinking..." He trailed off. "Well, here's the thing: I wondered if you'd be willing to take Frenchie for a few days."

"I thought you'd never ask." I held out my arms for the dog.

Chapter Ten

He immediately handed her over.

"Just until we can find more out about Colette and her family and decide what to do." The relief was clear on his face.

"You go get her stuff and I'll take her to the car."

I suddenly remembered it wasn't my car. "Do you mind?" I turned to Max.

"Not at all." He smiled. "I don't know what your cat's going to think of the idea, though."

"She'll be fine." I smiled back. "It's Mrs. Pickett next door I'm more worried about." Ernest rarely went outside, so he skated under the radar most of the time. With Frenchie, that wouldn't be the case, and I could guarantee there would be some issue.

Theo must have had Frenchie's things packed and at the ready, because he was back in a flash. I set the carrier in the back seat of Max's Land Rover and placed the dog inside while rubbing her head and talking to her. Using the seat belt to secure the carrier, I slipped her a treat.

"Let's try this," I told her. "You'll be okay there."

"There's extra food in here." Theo handed me the bright pink tote I'd seen in Colette's room. "And I put one of Colette's sweaters in the carrier with her. Colette said sometimes she did that when she had to take Frenchie to the vet. She thought it comforted her so I thought it was worth a try." He shrugged.

"We'll get on just fine." I gave the guy a hug. "Let me know when you find Colette's family and need me to bring her back." In my heart I had doubts that finding Colette's family was going to come that quickly, but I could certainly be flexible.

"I really appreciate this." He pushed dark hair off his forehead and I thought I spotted a new Band-Aid on his hand.

I settled myself in the front seat for the drive back. Max had a great sense of direction and seemed fine with navigating the way back. He made exactly the correct turn out of the driveway and in a short time we were on the road to St. Ignatius.

"What did you think after meeting the family?" I asked.

"An interesting bunch." He glanced over at me. "I gather you don't think the death of the girl was an accident."

"I was hoping for it." I turned to look back at Frenchie, who'd settled into the carrier and was asleep, her nose buried in the soft blue sweater Theo had tucked in. "But things don't add up. Gwen told me the woods surrounding the bed-and-breakfast are clearly posted *No Hunting*."

"That should be enough, but I have signs up also and sometimes it's not." Max lived in an old farmstead that he'd bought and had several acres of woodland near the house. "Last year I ran off some young hunters that had either not seen the signs or had seen them and ignored them."

"It seems odd that Colette has no family contacts, though." I glanced out at the countryside that sped by. Rolling grassy hills, wildflowers, fields of corn ready for harvest. "Sheriff Terry said her emergency info was fake. Theo knows nothing about her family. They can't find anyone who knows anything about her past. It seems weird, you know."

"Weird, maybe." Max stopped at a dusty stop sign and turned onto the highway that would take us home. "But it still could be accidental. I mean, no one was around but the family and what reason would any of them have to get rid of Colette?"

"I know." I shook my head. "It doesn't make sense. One mystery solved this trip, though."

"What was that?" he asked.

I explained about seeing someone outside and finding the cigarette butt and now discovering it was Marta's.

"Well, that was a surprise."

"It certainly was," I agreed. "I'll call the sheriff tomorrow."

We were quiet for a mile or two and then I remembered I'd wanted to ask Max about Libby.

"The girl, Libby—you ran into her in the woods?" I asked.

"Yes, she was taking photos and didn't realize she was on private property." He nodded.

"What was she taking photos of?"

"I'm not sure," he responded. "Nature shots, I guess."

"Did she say why she was in the area? Or how she found her way to the Arbor property?"

"No." Max glanced over at me and smiled. "You have a very suspicious mind."

"I do," I agreed. "But you have to admit, it seems a bit funny that she appeared out of nowhere."

I leaned back in my seat and enjoyed the pleasure of being able to relax and look out the window. Fields of crops were an endless wave on both sides of the road. Almost ready for harvest.

Maybe my father's family had been farmers. According to Lucinda, there were limited options for the original settlers to the state, so it was likely farming unless they came much later. Perhaps they lived in an area like this. I looked forward to Lucinda sharing more about how to research family roots. She'd given me a place to start and I couldn't wait to dive on my own research in the first chance I had.

But first the Arbor family cookbook.

* * * *

We arrived back in St. Ignatius before the sun had gone down. The days were getting shorter and soon it would be dark by eight or nine o'clock.

Max pulled into my driveway and came around to help me carry Frenchie and her things inside.

I unlocked the door and flipped on some lights so we could see better. Ernest immediately appeared from the kitchen, where I'm sure he had been enjoying one of his favorite pastimes, watching his food dish.

He meowed a loud complaint about being left alone for so long.

"I think you're in trouble." Max chuckled and reached down to pick up Ernest. "Hi, buddy." He scratched under the cat's chin and then put him back down on the floor.

"It sounds like it." I set down Frenchie's carrier and she stood up, looking around in confusion.

"Have you had a dog and a cat in the same house before?" Max asked.

"Before moving here, I'd never had a pet." I knelt down and stuck my finger through the gap in the wire front to pet Frenchie's nose. "Not a dog or a cat or a goldfish. My mother wasn't a fan and when I was out on my own, I was always too crazy busy."

I flipped open the latch on the door of the carrier.

"Well, you might want to—" Max began.

Too late.

Frenchie shot out and ran in circles around the room. Her high-pitched, excited barking echoed off the walls. Ernest arched his back and hissed, his tail suddenly twice its normal size. He leaped onto the nearby entry table, knocking off a vase and scattering mail everywhere. Frenchie lunged forward, barking at the pieces of the vase.

I tried to grab the poodle and missed as she jumped sideways. Ernest took that opportunity to dive from the table to the floor and then under the couch. Frenchie followed, still barking, wedging her nose under the side.

Ernest hissed a warning, then struck. I didn't think his claws actually connected with her nose, but Frenchie let out a piercing screech and scuttled back to her carrier. Ernest shot out from under the couch and headed upstairs in a furry flash.

I looked at Max. "You were saying?"

He grinned. "I was saying you might want to let them get acclimated to each other. It doesn't always go well."

"No kidding."

I got Frenchie to come back out of the carrier and checked her over. There was no bleeding so I think she was more startled than injured.

After Max left, I cleaned up the broken vase. Thank goodness it was an inexpensive find from a yard sale and not some fancy high-priced item my mother had sent me.

I gathered the mail that had gone every which way. Then I went upstairs to see if I could find Ernest. He was sitting on top of my dresser, still on high alert, a look of betrayal on his face. I picked him up, but he refused to relax. He didn't take his eyes off the bedroom door, watching to make sure we weren't attacked again.

"We have to get along with each other," I told him. "Frenchie is our guest. She has lost her person and we're going to let her stay here for a while."

He jumped out of my arms and headed for the bathroom, where he waited for me to join him and turn on the faucet so he could get a drink. I didn't know why he insisted on drinking water that way when his water dish in the kitchen was always filled with fresh water. Which reminded me that I'd better check on his food. He had been alone most of the day and I generally give him more food when I get home from work.

Back downstairs, I looked around for Frenchie and didn't see her. I flipped on the light in the kitchen and found her right away. She'd polished off Ernest's food and was now helping herself to his water. She looked up at me, water dripping from her face and chin, giving her a bewildered Fu Manchu poodle appearance. Apparently all the excitement had made her very thirsty.

Ernest looked at us from the doorway.

"Sorry, bud." I reached down to get the dishes and set them in the sink to wash them out. I'd have to sort out this feeding thing. I grabbed Frenchie's bag from the living room and headed back to the kitchen to find a bowl for her food.

She stood in the middle of a room in a puddle.

Ernest gave a loud meow as if to comment on what he thought about our guest.

No good deed goes unpunished.

That's what my Aunt Cricket would say and, in this case, it wasn't far from the truth.

I guess there was more to dog-sitting than I'd realized. Max had been right to ask about my experience. It consisted of interactions with Dixie's dog, Monto. She sometimes brought him to the office. He mostly napped and begged treats.

I grabbed some paper towels and cleaned up the puddle. Ernest walked out of the room, his tail switching in disgust.

Finding Frenchie's leash and clipping it on, I took her outside. We walked north. Or maybe south. Anyway, we walked in the opposite direction from Mrs. Pickett's house. There were lights on and she was probably inside with her television on, but somehow the woman always knew when something had gone awry at my house. Then she would show up at my door. I didn't think I was up to dealing with her tonight.

We walked three blocks and then turned back. Frenchie seemed happy with the arrangement, trotting along beside me, occasionally stopping to sniff a plant or water one.

When we got back home, Ernest had situated himself on the back of the chair where I usually sat to read. He raised his head, but other than that seemed settled. I unclipped Frenchie and she jumped up on the couch and lay down.

Things were looking up.

I left the two of them in their living room détente and went to clean up Ernest's dishes. Running water in the sink and washing them thoroughly, I rinsed the two bowls and set them aside to dry. Looking around, I tried to figure out where I could put them that Frenchie couldn't reach but Ernest could.

I hated to put them on the counter because I'd been trying to train Ernest to stay off the counter. It was, however, the most likely solution, as there was a ton of counter space. The big country kitchen was one of the things I loved about the house. It was currently a rental, but I hoped to someday be able to buy it. Greer Gooder, my landlady, had also become a good friend.

I slapped my forehead. How could I have forgotten? I was supposed to call Greer when we got back. She lived in town at the Good Life, a retirement community, and she would be upset if I didn't stop by and fill her in on the latest at Arbor House. Mostly she'd be upset if the other residents had more of a scoop than she did.

I called Greer's number but the call went directly to voicemail. Glancing at my watch, I realized she was probably at Scrabble night. Greer loved all the activities at the Good Life, but her two favorites were movie night and Scrabble night at the community center. I'd try her again tomorrow morning.

I filled the dishes and placed them in the middle of the table. Maybe tomorrow I'd be able to come up with a better idea.

"I'm going upstairs," I announced to the two as I went through the living room. I wasn't sure how Frenchie would do in a strange house, but she seemed to regard her carrier as her safe place, so maybe she was used to sleeping there.

As I got ready for bed, I was sure I'd have trouble falling asleep. But I was out minutes after my head hit the pillow.

* * * *

I woke up on the very edge of the bed, with Ernest curled in the small of my back and a black poodle nose inches from my face.

"Good morning, Frenchie." She was just tall enough to reach the side of the bed if she stood on her hind legs.

The integration of feline and canine seemed to have improved. Or at least no one was hissing or barking. Progress.

I tried to sit up without mashing the cat and he finally moved, but not without giving me a very stern look. Switching his tail, he jumped to the nightstand, tried to stick his paw in the bottle of water I'd left there, and then unable to do that, batted it off the edge so that the water bottle landed directly on Frenchie's head.

The poor pup yelped as if she'd been attacked by a wild animal. And I guess in a way she had, but it was a plastic bottle and only a tiny bit of water was left in it, so it hadn't been heavy.

"Ernest, be nice," I scolded, grabbing a towel from the laundry basket and mopping up the water that had spilled onto the floor.

Heading down the stairs, Ernest was with me every step of the way. Frenchie sat on the top step, watching forlornly.

"Come on, girl." I motioned for her to come ahead but she just stared down at me.

I looked behind me where Ernest sat, looking innocent.

I sighed and headed back up to get the dog.

Chapter Eleven

Dixie had already arrived when I got to the office. I pulled the Jeep in beside her pickup, which was parked in the shaded area behind the shop. Stepping inside, I set Frenchie's crate down in order to pull the door shut.

"How did it go?" She must have heard me come in. "Oh." She stopped.

"Yeah." I picked up the carrier and headed to my office. "Just temporarily. Until they can find out about Colette's family."

"I can only imagine how that went over with Ernest." Bending down, she unlatched the door and Frenchie pranced out. "Did you survive, sweetie?"

Why did everyone see that cat-dog issue coming but me?

"She did okay."

"I was talking to you." Dixie grinned up at me.

"I don't know what I was thinking, but I couldn't leave the poor pooch there with Theo trying to take care of her, and her nipping him at every chance."

"I get it. And if it's any consolation, I probably would have done the same." She picked up Frenchie and snuggled her. "How is the family holding up?"

"Pretty well, all things considered." I reached in and fluffed the sweater Theo had put in the carrier. It had been a good idea: The dog liked laying her head on it when she was in the crate. She probably could smell Colette on the fibers.

"Any news on the case?"

"Not really news, but some details to share." I booted up my computer and sat down. "Sheriff Terry had let Theo know they contacted the firm where she worked and that her emergency contacts were bogus."

"No other leads on his end?"

"None." I tried to take a sip from my travel mug and realized it was empty. A comment on my morning. "Let me get the coffeepot fired up and I'll fill you in on the rest."

I started the coffee and then filled Dixie in on the photos Max had taken, our invitation to stay for dinner, Libby, the mystery girl; the big Marta revelation, and how I'd come home with Frenchie.

"Wow, I feel like a slacker."

"Right," I scoffed. "You could never be a slacker."

It was part of the reason we worked so well together: We both believed in the virtues of hard work and getting things done.

"Maybe not a slacker, but I used to be better about not volunteering at every opportunity." She handed me the filled coffee cup. "You're a bad influence."

"Probably." I took a sip. "If you can't be an inspiration to people, be a warning."

"Your Aunt Cricket?" she asked.

"Always." I took another drink and set the cup on my desk. "What have you volunteered for now?"

"The quilting ladies over at Quilting Time are having an open house and I told them I'd donate some cookies."

"That's easy-peasy for you. I'm sure they'll be good."

"That's not the problem." She made a face. "The problem is I need for them to look like quilt squares. I have some ideas, but I'm not sure. Can you take a look?"

"Sure." I was happy to help on the design side of things. Dixie knew better than to ask me to help on the baking side.

After looking at her ideas for designs, I was even more sure the cookies would be perfect. We picked a simple square shortbread cookie for the base and all of the creative work was done with the frosting.

"Okay, then." Dixie pulled her dark red hair into a bun. A sure sign things were about it get serious in the kitchen. "I'm going to try a batch and then this afternoon, I'll practice frosting them."

"Great idea." I saw practice cookies in my future. And probably in Disco's future as well.

The design settled, Dixie went off to tackle her cookie-making.

I refilled my cup and then gave the sheriff a call before I dug in on the office work. Frenchie was perfectly happy to sit at my feet and without interruption, I was able to get a lot accomplished. I was surprised at the time, but more than ready for a break when Dixie popped back in and suggested lunch.

"Do you think Frenchie will be okay here on her own?" Remembering the chocolate mousse incident, I was concerned there were so many ingredients in the kitchen and the storeroom that might be harmful.

"Back in the carrier she goes." Dixie reached down and patted the dog. "But first, let's do a potty break."

"Good idea." I picked up the pink leash.

"I'll take her." Dixie held out her hand. "I don't mind."

"Thanks." I handed over the leash. "I'll shut down here."

They were back in a few minutes and Frenchie didn't fuss at all about going into her carrier. I slid the door closed and waved good-bye. We went out the front.

The Red Hen Diner was not even a full block away.

"Cluck" the door chime announced as we entered. "Cluck"—there were two more groups behind us. The diner was busy today. No surprise, really, as the food was a good as the chicken decor was kitschy.

We seated ourselves, sliding into a booth. The head chick, Toy herself, bustled over with two waters and lots of questions.

"What's the latest on the murder at Arbor House?" She slid into the booth beside Dixie.

"Like we said the other night, we don't even know for sure that it wasn't an accident." Dixie took a sip of her water.

"It could still turn out to be hunters," I added, reaching for the menu that Toy handed to me. "It might have been just a horrible accident."

"That's not what I heard." She handed another menu to Dixie.

"What did you hear?" I looked at her over the insert that listed today's Chicken-Lickin' Specials.

"I know you said the sheriff's still calling it a 'suspicious death.'" She actually did air quotes. "That sounds like a murder to me."

"They have to call it that until they can rule out foul play." I suddenly realized I sounded like I'd watched too many Mystery Channel shows.

"Right." She stood. "What'll you have?"

Dixie ordered the chicken fried chicken and I opted for crispy chicken club sandwich. I glanced at my step-tracker.

"Calculating how many steps to offset the club?" she asked.

"Guilty." I would take Frenchie on a walk when we got back to the office and after a few blocks of that she hopefully would be willing to nap the rest of the afternoon. Then when I got home, I'd take her out again. Maybe this situation, with having a dog I was responsible for walking, was just the ticket to keep me moving.

"When we get back, I'll call Gwen to check in and see if we can get something scheduled to go over the table of contents with them. I'd like to get it set because I've got that band group who want to see a proposal and I need to get that scheduled as well."

"A good problem to have, right?" Dixie shifted as Toy brought our drinks: iced tea for me and lemonade for Dixie.

"It is," I agreed.

It'd been slow going getting the business started, and now we were beginning to get some traction. Mostly referrals from previous clients, which was great. That meant that the cookbooks we'd done had been successful.

Our food arrived quickly. Another reason the Red Hen Diner was so successful. Great food and quick service. Toy stopped by to refill our drinks, but was thankfully too busy to stop with more questions.

"I keep thinking about the morning I found Colette," I said between bites.

"I know, Sugar. That must have been awful." Dixie stopped her fork halfway to her mouth.

"It was," I agreed. "But that's not what I mean. I keep trying to remember where everyone was at the time."

"You're still leaning toward family members if it doesn't turn out to be an accident?"

"The place is so isolated, who else could it be?" I put my sandwich down. "If there'd been any strangers around, the local folks would have noticed."

"You mean like that Shorty guy?" Dixie asked.

"Exactly."

"As far as the family members go, I don't know why they'd want to kill the grandson's fiancée, but not everyone was up at that time of day."

"You're right." I remembered the siblings, J.J., Jezzie, and Jonathan were all in the downstairs porch area and I'd told Sheriff Terry that. "Who was up?"

"I hadn't left our room yet, so I don't really know."

"When Jonathan had me come upstairs, Gwen and Hilda were in the kitchen. I didn't see Theo or Lucinda."

"Still." Dixie cut a bite-sized piece of her chicken. "No reason to want her dead."

"You're right, of course." I picked up my sandwich again, a challenge as the layers were thick and the lettuce kept sliding out. "It's got to be an accident. That's all there is to it."

We didn't stick around too long at the diner because we didn't want to tie up a booth when they were so busy. Once we were done, we paid and headed back across the square to Sugar and Spice Cookbooks.

Back at the office, I took Frenchie for her walk, heading away from the square so that we could stretch our time a bit.

My tracker showed we were racking up the points and, in fact, at this pace I'd be able to have one of those quilt cookies

The afternoon went quickly as Dixie finished off her cookies for the Quilting Time folks, and I worked on laying out the sections of the Arbor family cookbook and sorting out which recipes she was recommending for photos.

We usually did photos of the various dishes for section breaks. Doing pictures with more recipes drove up the printing costs and most of our projects were fundraisers. But not this time. In this case, I wondered about using family photos for the different chapters. I couldn't wait to see what Max had come up with from the formal pictures. Once I'd seen those, I'd have a better idea.

I made a few phone calls. Letting Liz know what I had in mind and listening to her suggestions, made the Arbor House project clearer in my mind. I also took a call from another group, this one a sorority, with an interest in getting pricing on doing a cookbook.

When Dixie had a break, I asked her to come and take a look at what I'd laid out and with a few changes we decided on breaking the book into: the Quiche That Started It All, Breakfast and Brunch, Soups and Lunches, Family Dinners, and Desserts. Five simple sections. We had enough recipes to have six or seven in each of the chapters, with the exception of the first one. It seemed only right since the business had been started with quiche that it star in its own section.

I hoped the family would be okay with the inclusion of family photos. The cookbook's purpose was to preserve family recipes and the pictures would help tell that story. I still thought there might be some commercial appeal, but that wasn't what they'd hired us to do, so I'd leave that decision up to them.

* * * *

Arriving home, I dropped my mail on the table, hoping it was safe from flying cats this time. Ernest sat on the staircase watching me. I set down the crate and opened it so Frenchie could get out. She stayed inside.

"Okay, whenever you're ready." I reached inside and rubbed her head.

Parking my handbag and my briefcase by the couch, I headed to the kitchen to see what I could find for dinner. It would be nothing as elaborate as what we'd had at Arbor House the day before, that was for sure.

First off, my cupboards and my refrigerator were pretty bare. With the previous weekend at the B and B, I hadn't shopped for groceries.

Secondly, my cooking skills leave a lot to be desired. Dixie is the cook in the business and thank goodness for that. I can make a mean grilled cheese or a hardy Crock-Pot chili, but the fancy recipes we collected were beyond my skill set.

I looked through the pantry and finding nothing for inspiration, opted for the aforementioned grilled cheese.

I filled Ernest's dish while my sandwich was grilling. Then I opened a can of Frenchie's special food and put it in her dish. She must have recognized the sound because she trotted into the kitchen, her nails clicking on the floor.

Ernest followed, keeping to the outside of the room, sliding against the wall, and then leaping to the table when I wasn't looking.

"Enough drama, you two." I flipped my sandwich and got out a plate.

After I'd cleaned up my dishes, I got out my notes from the time I'd spent with Lucinda talking about genealogy. At her suggestion, I looked into some online resources. The website that helped locate graves was fascinating. I looked up the cemetery Dixie and I had discovered down the road from Arbor House.

Talk about a rabbit hole, by the time I came up for air it was way past my bedtime and my eyes were blurry from all the screen time. I made a few notes about some sites I wanted to follow up on, shut down my computer, and headed upstairs to get ready for bed.

* * * *

When I came downstairs the next morning, Frenchie was waiting by the door expectantly. She had adapted to her new routine pretty quickly. I had not. I couldn't walk the dog in my pajamas.

I'd developed a habit of coming downstairs and starting the coffee, plopping down in a chair to wait for it, and having a bit of wake-up time with my cat and my coffee. Waiting for the caffeine to kick in.

From the dance Frenchie was doing at the front door, that was not an option.

"Hang on just a minute," I told her. "I'll be right back."

I dashed back upstairs and threw on some clothes, hurried back down, clipped on her leash, and headed out.

Ernest watched balefully from my chair.

What, no cuddle time?

The message was as clear as if he'd said it aloud.

"Sorry." I blew him a kiss. "We'll be right back."

After a quick walk down the block and back, Frenchie and I headed back to the house.

I opened the door and walked in. Ernest looked up, a shredded tangle of light blue yarn in his mouth.

"Oh, no, Ernest. What do you have?"

It was the blue sweater from Frenchie's crate and Ernest was dragging what was left of it across the floor. He would drag and then pounce on it, claws out, like it was a big blue fluffy mouse. The sweater unraveled more with each pounce.

"Oh, no, you don't. That is not yours." I lunged for the sweater, tangling myself in Frenchie's leash and skidding on my knee across the floor.

I came to a halt, rubbing my knee, which was okay, except for an angry rug burn.

"Ernest, you are in big trouble." Picking up the remains of the sweater, I checked it over.

Angora wool, the label said. Probably expensive, like Theo's Italian leather shoes.

It had been kind of a shame to use something so beautiful as a comfort item for a dog, but I was sure Colette would have been fine with it.

I held it up. Greer was a knitter; maybe she could help me piece it back together. As I got to the part that was still intact, it was heavier than I thought it would be. I patted it down and realized there was a coin purse tucked in the pocket.

"Well, that would do it," I said to the two animals who were now watching me closely— Frenchie by my side, Ernest from across the room. I opened the clasp of the coin purse and peered in. A few coins, a single earring, and a folded piece of notebook paper. Expecting a grocery list, I unfolded the paper.

YOU CAN'T RUN FOREVER. I WILL NEVER STOP HUNTING YOU.

Bold letters marched across the page.

I dropped the note.

Scrambling to my feet, I grabbed my phone, dropped it, picked it up and dialed Sheriff Terry.

As I waited for him to answer, I tried to figure out who might have been threatening Colette, if Theo had known anything about the threats—and, also, how I was going to explain why the note was in my possession.

Chapter Twelve

I made some coffee and poured myself a cup. I carefully moved the note from the floor to the table using salad tongs from the kitchen.

I knew I'd already handled it, but I didn't want to make things worse. I hadn't gone upstairs to change, afraid to damage the note by carrying it around and afraid to let it out of my sight. Who knew what my Animal House companions might do if left them unattended?

The knock on the door made me jump, even though I'd known Terry was on his way. I let him in and led him to the kitchen table.

"It's right there." I pointed. "You can use the tongs if you want."

He picked it up by the edge and read it. "And it was where?"

"Inside a coin purse in the pocket of Colette's sweater." I pointed at the pile of blue knit that had been a sweater and the coin purse that I'd placed on the table beside the note.

"And you have Colette's sweater why?" He dropped the note on the table.

"Because Theo thought it might help Frenchie," I explained. "You know, something with Colette's scent to comfort the dog."

"I hate to ask, but how in the Sam Hill did you end up with the dog?" His cheek twitched and I could tell he was resisting a grin.

I explained about Theo and the biting and the shoes. And no one at Arbor House really being interested in the dog.

"It's just until they can figure things out," I finished.

"Okay, back to the sweater." Terry shook his head. "We went through all of her personal effects looking for any clues about her family. I don't understand how forensics missed this."

I'd been thinking about that while I'd waited for the sheriff to arrive. "Before you dress down the forensics crew, consider this: When I helped

Hilda pack up Colette's room I didn't see this sweater. That makes me wonder if Theo hadn't taken it and put it in with the dog before they arrived on the scene."

"I told the family not to touch anything." He paused. It was clear they hadn't taken his request all that seriously. I imagined he was wondering what else they'd ignored.

"Coffee?" I asked.

"Please." He placed his knuckles on the table, leaned over the note, and looked at it again. "It could be male or female. It's hard to tell with the printing."

I handed him the cup. "I'm guessing the note sort of makes it seem less likely that Colette's death was accidental."

"Yep." He took a gulp of coffee. "It sure does."

He picked up the coin purse and dumped out the coins, the solitary earring, and a necklace I hadn't noticed when I'd fished out the note.

He held it up by the chain to look at it and I felt my heart clutch.

I'd seen a necklace just like that not but a day ago. It was just like the half-heart necklace that the photographer, Libby, had worn.

It could be a coincidence, but…

Once I was able to speak, I filled Terry in on the girl, Libby, who'd been at Arbor House, what I could remember of her appearance, and the fact that she'd been upstairs a little longer than seemed necessary. And that I couldn't prove it, but I thought she'd been in a room other than the bathroom.

"The family didn't know her?" he asked.

"No one acted like they did. Max talked to her more than anyone," I told him. "They were out walking around taking photos and then they also conversed about photography. It seemed like she was pretty knowledgeable, not like it was just a cover, but who knows."

"I'll give Max a call." Terry dropped the necklace back in the coin purse and then bagged all the items.

* * * *

After the sheriff left, I called Dixie and filled her in, letting her know I'd be a bit late into the office. Then I showered and dressed. I was packing up and getting ready to head out when my cell phone rang.

It was Greer.

"How nice to hear from you." I suddenly remembered that the last time we'd talked we'd made plans for lunch.

Good grief, what day was it?

"I was calling to check and see if we were still on for lunch today."

I could picture her in my mind. Like me, she was also probably on her second or third cup of coffee. She'd be drinking hers from her favorite cup, a sunny yellow one with the words *Cup of Happy* on the side. That was Greer in a nutshell. Circumstances aside, she'd decided to be happy.

"Of course, we're on for lunch," I answered.

"I wasn't sure. I know you're busy." I could hear the click as she put her cup down. "I made that chicken salad that you like."

"Not too busy for lunch."

"That's great. I can't wait to hear about your latest investigation."

"They've not yet ruled it a murder. And I'm not investigating. But I'll fill you in at lunch."

"Great!" Her excitement came through the phone loud and clear.

"Do you mind if I bring a friend?"

"Not at all," she answered. "Is it the handsome Max?"

"No, this is a furry friend," I explained. "I'm dog-sitting a toy poodle and she doesn't do very well being left alone with Ernest."

"Sure, bring her along."

"Okay, I'll see you around noon."

I loved my lunches with Greer. Despite the gap in our ages we liked a lot of the same things and she was always so upbeat. I was in need of a good dose of upbeat about now.

* * * *

When I finally got to the office Dixie was champing at the bit to know what the sheriff had to say about the note.

I filled her in and then after settling Frenchie in the office, I got to work in an attempt to make up for my mostly lost morning.

There's nothing like a time crunch to up your productivity and I have to say by the time it came to leave for lunch with Greer, I'd probably accomplished more than I had in the past two days.

I'd written up three of the narratives to go with Arbor family recipes, saved my work to review later, and sent off a couple of email responses to potential clients.

"I'll be back," I called to Dixie, latching the door on Frenchie's carrier and grabbing my bag. "Call or text me if you need anything."

"Got it," she answered. "Have fun!"

* * * *

Frenchie was almost as excited as I was to be going to lunch at the Good Life Retirement Village. I felt bad that she'd spent so much time in her carrier, but it seemed to be her safe place. Maybe this outing would make up for her forced confinement a little bit.

I walked her every morning and every night. The morning walk was often brief, but the evening one was longer. I wasn't sure Ernest was going to get over his kitty funk over losing his morning partner for coffee-and-cuddle time any time soon.

Parking in the visitor lot, I headed across the way to Greer's unit. The one-story, brick four-plexes were arranged to provide access to the sidewalks while still maintaining a sense of privacy. Each had a patio out front and most of the residents had decorated them to varying degrees. Some with pots of sedate flowers, others with small statues or flags. One of my favorites was a small hobbit-like garden character placed amid some greenery. Several people were out walking, enjoying the warm fall day.

Frenchie trotted beside me, looking around, tail wagging. A couple of ladies stopped to pet her and say hello. The little pup was thrilled with the attention.

When we approached Greer's unit, I could see she was outside on her patio. She'd filled her flowerpots with hardy, bright yellow mums that matched her coffee cup. She stood as we approached. Her glasses were perched on top of her head, almost lost in her white curls.

"Well, hello there." She leaned over and scratched Frenchie's topknot. "What a sweet girl you are."

"Greer, meet Frenchie." I held out my hand toward my friend. "Frenchie, this is Greer."

The little dog pranced like she knew what I was saying, then sat on her haunches and held out her paw.

Greer shook it. "Nice to meet you."

I was dumbfounded. Who knew?

"I know you don't have a lot of time, so I have lunch ready for us." She opened the door and waved me in.

The inside of her place was as warm and friendly as Greer herself. The furnishings were comfortable and right-sized for the compact space. I wondered sometimes if she didn't miss her big house, but she claimed she didn't. But that was Greer. Get on with it. Move along. No regrets.

I followed her into the kitchen. "You didn't need to go to all this trouble."

"I didn't know you were getting a dog," she commented as she got the chicken salad out of the refrigerator and placed it on the counter.

"I wasn't."

Croissants had already been cut and placed on a plate and in a matter of minutes she had them filled and ready.

"Frenchie belonged to Colette," I explained. "The girl that was killed at Arbor House."

"Oh, my word." Greer stopped in her preparations. "Couldn't her family take the poor thing?"

"That's just it." I took a sip of the iced tea Greer handed me. "They can't find her family."

"Come here, little dog." Greer opened the fridge and took out some plain cooked chicken. She put it in a small dish and set it on the floor for Frenchie. "I had more than I needed for our chicken salad."

I'd only been giving her the fancy food that Theo had sent with her. I wasn't sure where to buy it so I'd hoped it would hold out for the length of her stay with me. But she seemed perfectly satisfied with Greer's plain cooked chicken. Again, who knew?

"Are you sure I can't help with anything?" I asked.

"No, you can't." She pointed to a chair. "Sit."

She washed her hands and joined me at the small dining table. "Okay, let's hear it. Who is this girl that was killed?"

"Her name was Colette, or we think it was. She was Theo, the grandson's fiancée," I explained. "They'd only arrived the night before."

"Hmm." Greer took a bite of the chicken salad sandwich. "This is good, if I do say so myself."

"It is," I agreed.

"So, you found her, huh?" She was back to Colette. "And what do you mean, you think that was her name."

"They can't find any relatives. The emergency contacts she had on file at the place she worked were phony. Sheriff Terry says fake names, fake numbers, fake addresses."

"That's odd," Greer mused. "Do you think her name was fake as well?"

"It sounds like they think it could be. They're not finding any history older than the past year."

"What about the Arbor people?" she asked. "Tell me about them."

I gave her a brief rundown on Marta, the siblings, their spouses, and Theo.

"He's the only grandchild?"

"That's right and doted on by Grandma, from what I could tell."

"I thought I'd have grandchildren." Greer sighed and looked out the window into the distance. "But Spencer is such a self-involved poop, I don't think he'll ever get married."

"Greer, he's not."

"Thanks for saying that, my dear, but he is. You do your best, but..." She shrugged her narrow shoulders. "I hold out hope that he'll wake up one day and realize that the world does not revolve around him."

I'd not had a good experience with her son. In fact, I'd had a really bad experience where he'd falsely accused me, but I didn't hold it against him. Still, I couldn't see how someone as nice as Greer could have a son as impossible as Spencer or Spiff, as everyone in town called him. He didn't live in St. Ignatius, but he wasn't that far away and the one thing I did hold against him was that he rarely had time to visit his mother.

"I blame myself." She used a fork to nudge some of the chicken salad back into the croissant.

"It's not always the parent's fault." I stopped to take a drink of my tea.

"Not completely," she agreed. "But as a mother you can't help but wonder where you went wrong."

We were quiet for a few minutes.

"Maybe if Spencer never gets married and never has kids..." She paused, looking at me over the rim of her glass, her eyes dancing. "Maybe you'll get married and have a bunch of kids and bring them over to see me."

"Nothing in the near future." I laughed.

"Speaking of which." She grinned. "How is the handsome Max?"

"I don't think we were speaking of him. But he is fine. He took a trip with me to Arbor House to get some photos of the family members."

"This cookbook is going to be quite the big deal then, huh?"

"It is, kind of." I took a deep breath. "I'm truly proud of the work we've done to curate the recipes and work in the family stories. I'm polishing that up and tomorrow Max is to come by the shop and shoot some more photos. This time of particular dishes."

"What kinds of things?" Greer folded her hands. "I'll bet there's some good recipes."

"There are. Dixie went through the family recipe cards that Marta, the mother, had written out through the years. There are quite a few classics—meat loaf, pot roast, and, of course, their signature quiche."

"Oh, right." Greer nodded. "That's what they're famous for, isn't it?"

"It is." I nodded. "I think the cookbook has a wider appeal than simply a family keepsake, but I don't think any of them feel that way."

"Well, maybe they don't want us cooking our own meals." She refilled our glasses. "They want us buying Arbor family frozen meals."

"I guess you're right. They've made quite a success of their family recipes over the years."

"They've done well," Greer agreed. "Seems like I read something or saw something about them on TV a while back."

"Really?" I stopped with the glass partway to my mouth. "What was it about?"

"I can't remember. Maybe something about laying off people. Or maybe something about people getting sick from their food. Maybe some people got salmonella poisoning? Or maybe I've got them mixed up with a different company." She tapped her temple. "With my memory, who knows?"

There was nothing wrong with Greer's memory. I'd have to check out a news story involving Arbor Family Foods. It didn't ring a bell with me, but I'd been so wrapped up in the startup of Sugar and Spice the past year that I'd sort of had tunnel vision.

"I'll check that out."

"Now let's get back to this dead girl." Greer began to gather our empty dishes. "And then Max while we have dessert. I want to hear about how things are going with Max."

I filled her in on Colette and shared the most recent development about the necklace. I begged off any Max updates, not because I was being coy but because, despite rumors to the contrary, there wasn't really anything to tell.

* * * *

When I got back to the office, the sheriff was sitting at the counter out front talking with Dixie. I could hear them laughing as I came in the back.

That made me smile. They'd come a long way from being all prickly with each other over a longtime-passed misunderstanding, to enjoying each other's company.

Setting Frenchie's crate down in my office, I rubbed my arm muscles. Not only was I getting extra steps as a result of my dog-sitting, I was getting a serious workout of my biceps.

As I walked out front, I noted the sheriff had one of the quilt square cookies in his hand.

"Those turned out really well." I pointed to the cookie. "Where are the rest?"

"I took them to the quilt ladies, but there were a few rejects." She pulled a plate out from under the counter. "I got too much bright blue on these."

"Very tasty rejects, though," Sheriff Terry added, taking another bite.

I tried not to stare at his blue lips, but sometimes my sense of humor gets stuck in middle school. And the sight of the very serious sheriff with Cookie Monster blue lips had me trying to hold back a snicker.

"Disco has already been by, but I saved a few for you." Dixie pushed the plate toward me.

"I'm not sure I have room after Greer's lunch." I took one anyway.

"How was Greer?" Dixie asked.

"Good." I bit into the cookie, pretty sure my lips were now also blue. "She mentioned some trouble Arbor Foods had a while back. Either labor related or associated with food safety. Do you remember hearing anything on the news?"

"I do kind of remember a story on the news a while back, now that you mention it." Terry munched on his cookie, his lips now an even brighter blue. "I don't think it's relevant to our murder investigation, though."

"No, probably not." I hunted for a napkin or paper towel to help us both with our cookie-induced lip stains. "I thought it was interesting was all. I didn't remember seeing it."

"Terry was telling me he talked to Max about the girl that may have a connection to Colette." Dixie handed me a roll of paper towels.

"Was he able to help you at all?" I tore off a section and scrubbed at my lips and then handed the roll to Terry.

"Not much." He took the paper towels but looked confused.

I pointed to my lips.

"He said she asked a lot of questions about the Arbor family, but he didn't share anything with her because he didn't know that much about the family." He handed the roll of towels back to me.

"Max mentioned to me when we were driving back that he thought it was a little strange that she'd picked that area to photograph when there are so many interesting spots around the state, but I guess he didn't ask her about it." I wished I'd said something to her when I thought she'd been snooping around upstairs. So much for my undercover work, huh?

"I'm headed up to the motel in Dewersville this afternoon to see what they've got as far as credit card records for her stay." Terry stood. "If she paid cash, I'm out of luck, but I'm hoping somewhere she used credit and then we'll have something to go on."

"You may want to see if you can get that blue food coloring off your lips before you go." I handed him back the paper towels. "If you want them to take you seriously, anyway."

I headed to my office to finish up some tasks. We'd planned the food photo shoot with Max for the following morning and I wanted to make sure we had the list printed out and that both he and Dixie had copies.

Frenchie looked up when I entered and then put her head back down. As much as I liked the pooch, this wasn't really a life for her, either. I wondered if the mystery girl would be a connection to Colette's family. I also wondered if she would know anything about the threatening note that had been in the coin purse with the necklace.

* * * *

I arrived at the office the next morning in plenty of time to get us set up for Max's photo shoot. Dixie was already on-site and had begun the cooking process.

I locked the front door and put up a *closed* sign to discourage interruptions. Mostly to discourage Disco, but also onlookers. We'd learned when Max did a photo shoot that the big front window of the shop attracted viewers, which defeated the purpose of using the area for its great lighting.

Max arrived shortly and began setting up his equipment. Unlike the photo shoot at Arbor House, these photos were all carefully staged. He'd brought extra lighting and different lenses for various views.

Because quiche was the dish that got the family business started it seemed like the proper place to start. Dixie had used the family recipe of basic quiche Lorraine and the smells coming from the kitchen were heavenly.

Not only a great cook, Dixie was a blue-ribbon baker, having won numerous first-place awards at the Iowa State Fair. That meant that in addition to making dishes that tasted good, she also had perfected the attention to detail on the presentation.

She came from the back carrying the quiche with the red silicone hot pads I'd bought her for her birthday.

"I didn't cut it because I wasn't sure what you wanted to do with it." She placed the white porcelain quiche pan on the counter. "I brought a knife in case you wanted to cut a piece out."

"Let's try it both ways." Max adjusted his camera and the lighting. "I'll take a few photos before we cut it and then we'll try some others with a single slice."

"That will be good, because it really needs to cool a bit before you cut into it." She fanned herself with one of the hot pads.

"It's really pretty, Dixie," I noted, leaning in to look at the dish. "And it smells incredible."

"Sugar…" Max's voice held a warning.

"I know." I backed up. "But when you're done taking photos, I'm having a slice of that."

He smiled.

"Have you heard how things are coming with the investigation?"

"There have been some developments." I took another step back to make sure I was out of the way.

He looked up from his camera with a raised brow.

Since finding the threatening note and then sending the sheriff his way, Max and I hadn't had a chance to talk.

"Once you're done with the shoot, I'll fill you in."

"Sounds good." He was back to full concentration on getting the right angle. He nudged the hot porcelain baking dish slightly, bunching the fabric, and angling the antique sterling silver server so it looked like brunch was ready.

Man, he was so talented. I loved this part, but I needed to stay out of the way.

"Maybe over some quiche," I said over my shoulder as I headed back to the office to check on Frenchie. And while I was there, I'd see what I could find on that news story Greer had mentioned.

When I sat down at my computer, the first thing I did was review some of the content I'd worked on the day before. I loved that the cookbooks we produced were, contrary to Marta's view, more than just a collection of recipes.

In my corporate days that hadn't been the case. It was all about product placement. I understood magazines needed to be profitable to stay in business, but I felt like sometimes the storytelling got lost.

The Arbor siblings thought this was a way to record their mother's recipes for future generations, but I wondered if there wouldn't be a wider market for it. Maybe the public would have an interest in the Arbor family recipes and the stories about them.

Maybe I was just fascinated with family stories because I didn't have any stories of my own. At least not on my dad's side. I knew his adoptive parents were from Iowa. They had both passed away shortly after my parents married. But that was it.

I polished up the pieces and then moved on to seeing if I could find that story about Arbor Foods.

It took some digging, but Greer had been right: There had been talks of layoffs at Arbor Foods. Not because of any health scare but because, at least according to the news story, the family was considering selling the company.

That didn't jibe with what Marta had said about Jezzie wanting to expand.

I printed off the story to give to the sheriff, although I was sure he and his team had done their own digging.

Chapter Thirteen

We'd assembled all the materials for the cookbook: the cover they'd picked, the mock-up Liz had created, the recipes we'd chosen. I'd slipped in a few tidbits from my chat with Marta. We had the latest photos from Max and had preliminary prints of the ones we were proposing to use. It was an impressive lot.

"I'm excited about how it's all coming together." I grinned at Dixie as we packed everything into a cardboard portfolio.

"I'm always a little amazed at this stage," she confessed. "It's a bit like a recipe you haven't tried. All the ingredients are there, but you aren't sure how it's going to come out until you stir them all together."

"I always have faith any recipe you try is going to turn out."

"I know you do." She squeezed my shoulder. "And I always have faith any cookbook we do is going to turn out because you're the best partner ever."

"The feeling is mutual."

I tried not to get choked up.

"All right then, let's see if the Arbor family is as impressed with our work as we are." I finished putting the last of the materials in the portfolio.

"If not, they can kiss—"

"Dixie Spicer!"

"What?" She laughed. "Grits! I was going to say *grits*. But anyway, we've worked hard on this and it's good work."

Carrying everything out to the Jeep, I slid everything behind the seat. And we climbed in and buckled up for the drive to Arbor House.

Setting my GPS, I pushed route.

"Starting route to Arbor House Bed-and-Breakfast," Matilda announced in her pleasant British accent.

"Really?" Dixie turned and looked at me. "You've been there how many times?"

"A few." I patted the GPS unit. "Don't listen to her, Mattie. You know we need each other."

To be honest, the drive did look very familiar and I might have been able to do it without Matilda's help, but there were a couple of times when I'd been sure she was going to say "turn left" and she'd announced a right turn.

Though my rose-colored glasses had been tarnished by all that had transpired since our weekend there, that first view of Arbor House when I made the turn into the driveway still enchanted me.

Nestled among the trees and framed by flowers, it was the perfect retreat. It had been spring when I'd come to talk to Gwen about that first project for the Iowa chapter of the Bed-and-Breakfast Association. The pastel flowers that had surrounded the graceful Victorian then had made it seem like a fairy house.

But now, the grove of trees had become a profusion of red and gold with the changing season, and the soft cream of the house almost glowed in the autumn light. The baskets of flowers on the wide porch had been switched to bunches of purple fountain grass and clusters of deep burgundy, rusty orange, and vivid yellow mums. It was breathtaking in a whole different way.

And who knew that first project would lead to this current one, a family project, which in spite of the tragedy and troubles they were going through, I still believed in. The ingredients were all there.

My glow lasted only from the parking lot to the front entrance.

As I raised my hand to knock, the heavy wooden door flew open and Tom brushed past us, Jezzie on his heels.

"I am out of here," he shouted, his face red. "I can't stand your family another minute. They make me sick!"

"Get back here." Jezzie reached out as she slammed the door shut behind her. "I need to talk to you about—"

Suddenly they both saw us and she stopped.

Tom hesitated for only a moment and then kept going. He didn't look back, but jumped in the powder blue Corvette and peeled out of the parking lot, throwing gravel.

I'd wondered who that car belonged to, but it had never seemed appropriate to ask.

"Sorry," I coughed from the rock dust in the air. I cleared my throat and tried again. "Sorry. We'd talked to J.J. and he said today would be a good time."

"Well, of course, he'd never tell me," Jezzie bit out, yanking open the door. "He's large and in charge all of a sudden."

She stopped, her back to us, and took a deep breath.

When she turned around, I could see the threat of tears in her dark eyes, but she straightened her shoulders and gave a strained smile.

"I am so sorry." She took another deep breath. "That was totally unfair, to take my upset out on you. We've had a lot going on the past two days and I'm afraid we're all on edge."

She held open the door. "Come in. I'll find out where the rest of the family is."

I didn't say anything, but knew where J.J. was. I'd spotted him standing at the edge of the house when Tom barged out. I wasn't sure how much he'd heard, but I was almost certain he'd heard the large-and-in-charge comment.

Glancing that way before I stepped inside, I didn't see him. He'd disappeared.

Jezzie went off to look for her siblings. Dixie and I made our way to the dining room table, which seemed like the easiest place to lay out the mock-up and the photos. As we were in the middle of unpacking the materials, Gwen came in.

"Oh, good you're here." She beamed a smile. As usual, her soft, sophisticated look made her seem elegant and approachable. The polished, yet casual, knit dress today was a dove gray and set off her silver curls. "We're looking forward to seeing what you've got for us."

Apparently, J.J. had told some of the family, just not Jezzie.

"Have you seen anyone else?" she asked.

"Jezzie was here and went to find everyone," Dixie answered.

"Hello." Lucinda came down the stairs. In contrast to Jezzie's polish and Gwen's quiet elegance, Lucinda always looked like she'd put on whatever was at hand. Today that had been a green sweater and a khaki-colored skirt that, though they were both green, somehow clashed.

"I'm so glad to see you both. Should I go up and get Mother Arbor?" She looked to Gwen.

"It sounds like Jezzie's already on it," Gwen said over her shoulder as she went through toward the kitchen. "I'm going to ask Hilda to bring us some iced tea and lemonade. Doesn't that sound good?"

"It does." Jonathan had come in from the front hallway. He leaned in and gave Gwen a peck on the cheek.

Jonathan approached the table and looked over my shoulder at the photos I was laying out one by one. Dixie had put the recipes in order so they could see how they would appear in the book.

"This is a great family photo." He picked up the print of the photo Max had taken of the whole group on the front porch. "Look at this." He held it up so J.J., who'd just come in from the back, could see it.

J.J. came forward and took it from him. "It is nice." He handed it off to Lucinda, who agreed.

"Careful, Grand-mère." Theo supported his grandmother as she made her way slowly down the stairs. She still had a bandage around her ankle. I wondered if she'd ever fessed up about sneaking outside.

When they reached the bottom, J.J. and Jonathan took over from Theo and helped get her settled in a comfortable chair. Once she was situated, she held up her hand.

"Let me see it," she commanded. "I could hear you all talking about it as I was coming down the stairs. Let me see the photo."

Lucinda handed it to Theo, who took it over to his grandmother. She studied it silently before handing it back to Theo.

"It is a good photo of us." I detected a bit of a quaver in her voice.

Who could blame her? It was a great capture of everyone together. Her whole family.

"Well, let's get on with this." She dabbed at the corner of her eye with a white hanky that had been tucked in her sleeve. "Is everyone here? Where are Jezzie and Tom?"

"I'm here. Tom won't be joining us." Jezzie spoke from the living room doorway. She kicked off the light-toned heels she'd been wearing and swirled the glass of red wine in her hand.

If they had questions about why Tom wasn't there, or why Jezzie was drinking so early in the day, no one seemed inclined to ask.

"Then I think we're all here." Jonathan nodded.

"Okay, if everyone can gather around." I hesitated; that left Marta out. I looked to Gwen.

She caught on right away.

"Mother Arbor, could we move you closer to the table so you can see?"

"I can hobble to the table," she insisted, standing up, "with some help."

We got Marta situated so she could see and I began my explanation of how the cookbook would come together. We had suggestions on the recipes to include, and I explained why we'd chosen those. In most cases, it was because the recipe had been mentioned by one of the family members as reminding them of a childhood memory or a family gathering.

We'd selected a few photos from the ones they'd shared with us. Some Max had been able to scan and enhance the quality. We had wanted to include an image of a few of the handwritten recipe cards, but they didn't scan well and overall just didn't fit with the high-quality look we were going for.

I passed around the template and explained why Liz had recommended the layout. She'd played off the cover they'd chosen and it gave a nice cohesive look to the cookbook.

There were a few questions but overall, they seemed happy with what we had planned.

Almost there. Dixie made notes about a few adjustments to make.

"I'll leave with you the photos we're not using, but keep the other ones until we're finished just in case Max has to re-scan anything," I said.

"And I've put all the recipe cards you let us borrow in this envelope." Dixie held up the manila envelope. "If you'd like, I'm happy to refile them for you."

"I'll take them." Gwen held out her hand. "I'll gladly refile them, but Hilda and I would like to take a look first. There may be some we want to try out on the B and B guests."

Dixie handed her the envelope.

"When we're completely finished and everything is off to press, I'll bring you the rest of the photos."

"You could just drop them in the mail," Jezzie said, looking up from one of the photos.

My first thought was "Could she be any more done with us?" But what I said was, "I appreciate the offer, but I'd feel better if I handed them off in person."

"Well, I think we've got your comments captured." Dixie patted the notepad she'd been using.

"And we should have a finished product for you in a few weeks," I added. "I'll get you a final date in the next few days."

"Thank you for showing this to us. We appreciate it," J.J. said, looking around at the group. "It preserves a part of our family history."

There were nods from the rest.

"Speaking of history. Sugar, do you have time to take a look at the genealogy progress I've made?" Lucinda asked.

"I'd love to, but we don't have a lot of time today." I'd started gathering up the papers and photos. "I have a friend taking care of Frenchie while I'm gone."

"Good lord, we've taken over your life, haven't we?" Lucinda blurted out. "That's sort of the way the Arbor family works. They take you in and take over your life."

That earned her a hard look from all the siblings, but I didn't think she'd meant it in a derogatory way.

"What?" she shot back at the group. "They came to get some recipes and photos for a cookbook and they find themselves in the middle of a murder investigation. And Sugar here now has responsibility for a random poodle. I'm sure that was never in their business plan."

I wasn't sure how to respond. I truly didn't mind taking care of Frenchie, but I was learning that taking care of the dog was much different than taking care of a cat. As far as the murder investigation, I wasn't sure how much Sheriff Terry had shared about the most recent developments.

"Come on." Lucinda motioned to me. "I'll make it quick. I have some new thoughts for you on your search for your father's family."

I hesitated.

"Go ahead." Dixie waved me away. "I'll finish packing up."

I followed Lucinda up the stairs to the library and, like before, she had to move some papers so I could sit down.

"Here's what I wanted to give you." She handed me a manila envelope. "There are some copies of old records in there. Examples from my own family research. The kind of thing you want to hunt for as you access online court, census, and military records."

"Thanks so much for this." I'd been overwhelmed with where to start and this would help.

"You have a good head for this stuff and a great attitude about it." She continued moving papers as she talked. "Many people only want to deal with the good news they find. There's a tendency to ignore the negative. The truth is, if you dig into any family's history… well, let's just say some things you unearth will make you proud and others things not so much."

"It seems like a given." I tucked the envelope in my bag. "You have to take the bad with the good."

"One more thing. Have you ever thought about a DNA test?" she asked.

"I'm not sure what good that would do." I shook my head. "It would be different if I'd found potential family members and wanted to confirm them. But I don't even have a lead on my father's biological parents."

"That's just it." She continued moving papers around, obviously looking for something. "It might give you a lead."

"How so?" I asked.

"The companies that sell the DNA tests keep a large database with the information. Your DNA might match other DNA info in the database if any of your father's relatives have done the test."

"I'd have access to that information?" I hadn't considered that option.

"People choose whether to make their information available to others doing research, but it's a possibility," she explained. "A long shot, maybe. But a possibility."

"I see." I nodded. "It might give me a place to start."

"Exactly. I did mine a while ago, but I've ordered DNA kits for all the Arbor crew and had them shipped here. I'm afraid if they don't do it now while I'm here, they'll get busy and not get around to it."

"Do you think they're interested in finding out about their roots?" No one had ever mentioned an interest when Lucinda talked to me about it, and we'd often been in the larger group.

"No, I don't think they are all that much," she admitted. "But I hope they'll indulge me. I've found some interesting twists in their family history and once I'm through with my family, I'd like to get on with my work on the Arbor family."

"Thanks for telling me about it and thanks for this." I held up the envelope. "I truly appreciate it."

We made our way downstairs and then outside to where Dixie and the group were assembled on the porch. The wind had come up a bit, but it was still a nice, warm fall day. We watched as Sheriff Terry came down the drive, parked, and got out of his car.

He stopped at the bottom of the steps, a serious look on his face. His eyes landed on Dixie and his expression lightened, but just for a moment, then he was back to Mr. Law Enforcement.

"I have an update, but I'd like to say it once," he said. "Is everyone here?"

I looked around. J.J. was missing, as well as Theo and Marta. Lucinda had come outside with me and everyone else had already been on the porch. Well, except for Tom.

"I'll go get Theo," Jezzie said. "And Mother, if she'll come."

"J.J. is in the living room," Lucinda said. "I saw him when we came past. Would you tell him to come out here as you go by?"

"Sure," Jezzie answered, opening the door.

I stepped down off the porch, closer to Sheriff Terry. "Tom, Jezzie's husband, isn't here right now," I said quietly. "We'd stopped by to show everyone the cookbook layout." I said that part a little louder.

There was a bit of an awkward pause while everyone waited.

"I'll just get the mail while we're waiting." Lucinda started down the steps.

"Stay put," I told her. "I'll get it." I glanced down at my tracker. These travel days were not doing me any favors on reaching my walking goals. Here was a chance to make up a few steps. I'd bet it was at least two hundred steps to the mailbox at the end of the drive.

Taking off at a brisk pace, I headed across the parking lot and then down the white rock driveway. At the end, I glanced at my wrist. Okay, I had been overly optimistic. It was only seventy-three steps. Still, that would be 146 by the time I got back to the porch.

I flipped open the metal mailbox and peered in. It looked like the there was a ton of mail and some small packages.

Reaching in and wrapping my fingers around the mail, a couple of envelopes fell to the ground. I reached down to grab them before the wind blew them away. And—

BOOM!

There was a blinding flash and I flew backwards, landing on my backside in the ditch. There were faint sounds but the clanging in my ears drowned them out.

What the heck had happened?

I laid back and closed my eyes. Opened them. Closed them again. The grass was soft. Faces gathered around me but I couldn't make sense of what they were saying. Gwen pushed through and offered me a damp towel. Placing it over my face, I tried to sit up. It fell off and I fell back.

The faces returned. Dixie looked concerned. Sheriff Terry leaned in.

I tried to say I was okay.

Then there was nothing but blackness.

I woke up in the back of an ambulance, a young EMT taking my vitals.

"I'm okay." There, I finally got it said.

"I'll be the judge of that," he said, tucking a blanket around me and attaching a blood pressure cuff to my arm.

"How's she doing?" Sheriff Terry looked in.

The ringing in my ears had improved to the point that I not only could hear him, I could hear the babble of talk outside the ambulance.

"It appears all of her injuries are tertiary," the young man answered.

"Still, I think we should transport her and have her looked over." Terry nodded at him and started to walk away.

"Hey, I'm right here." I sat up. "No need to talk about me like I'm not present."

"Sorry." Terry turned back. "Sugar, it doesn't look like anything from the blast got you, but you may have a concussion."

"Sheriff, you need to come and have a look." In addition to the ambulance, it appeared a crime scene team had also arrived. A tall blond tech was motioning to the sheriff. "This way," she pointed. "You aren't going to believe this."

I shifted on the stretcher in order to see where they were going, but the EMT pressed my shoulder back down so I lay flat.

"No, you don't."

"What's your name?" I asked.

"Erik," he responded, tapping the name badge on his bright white shirt.

"Well, Erik, I'm sure that I'm okay. What's it going to take to get you to feel the same?"

"Let's start with this." He went back to the blood pressure cuff.

That was only the first of things Erik thought needed to be checked and, in the end, though I thought I was very persuasive, I couldn't convince Erik or the sheriff that I didn't need a trip to the ER.

Chapter Fourteen

The closest hospital was thirty minutes away.

Dixie said she would follow in my car and said she was sure once they looked me over, they'd let me go home. I was sure she was right.

We were both wrong. The ER doc concurred that I didn't have any direct injuries from the bomb. But because it was a strong enough blast to knock me down, he felt it was possible I had a concussion.

So, no going home for me. They wanted to keep me until morning to watch for any delayed effects. At the moment, I just had a headache and a sore backside from where I had landed.

Dixie called Greer for me, who agreed to keep Frenchie overnight. Ernest would be fine on his own. He'd be upset at the disruption of our routine. But he'd been upset about that since Frenchie arrived on the scene.

I urged Dixie to go on home.

"Okay, if you're sure you're all right." She gave me a hug. "It doesn't feel right leaving you here all alone."

"I'll be fine." Truthfully, my head was pounding and I hoped if I closed my eyes it would stop. I couldn't remember if they'd given me something for the pain or not.

"Can I get you some water or something else to drink before I leave?" she asked.

"I've got some." I pointed to the pitcher one of the nurses had dropped off. "When you come back tomorrow, you could bring me some clean clothes. Mine are sort of grass-stained."

I remembered lying on my back in the grass wondering what had happened.

"I'm on it." She gave a thumbs-up.

At some point, lying there in the grass, I'd realized the mailbox had exploded.

"By the way, what was it that blew all over the place when the mailbox blew up?" I asked.

"I guess some bills, some junk mail, and a bunch of DNA kits." She made a face.

"Oh, right." I nodded, which made my head hurt more. "Lucinda had mentioned she'd ordered DNA kits for the Arbor family."

"That's kind of strange."

"I don't know. She's so into it that she thinks everyone else is too. I gather she hasn't gotten much interest from her hubs and his siblings." I'd been glad to find someone with her avid interest and expertise to get me started.

"Okay, get going." I shooed Dixie out of the room. "You have my keys, right?"

"I do." She pulled them from her pocket and jangled them. "And I'll be back first thing tomorrow to collect you. Don't be too hard on the nurses, okay?"

"I won't," I promised.

I didn't think I had it in me to be a problem for anyone right now. I leaned my head back on the soft pillow and closed my eyes.

I'd almost drifted off when I remembered the tall blond crime scene tech who'd been excited to show something to the sheriff. What was that about? I should have asked Dixie.

Good grief, and the sheriff had been going to fill us in on something before I went to get the mail. That's why he had been there. How could I have forgotten?

They must have given me something for the pain because I noticed it was less than before. I tried to concentrate on what exactly the blond had said to Terry. Something he needed to see.

Then I was gone.

Chapter Fifteen

The doctor had been by early and signed my release. He said a nurse would be by with instructions for things I was to watch for once I went home. I hoped it was Nurse Jamie, who'd checked my vitals earlier. She was very efficient and I was more than ready to go home.

In fact, I was impatiently sitting in the visitor chair by the bed, waiting for either Nurse Jamie or Dixie to arrive, when there was a tap on the door.

It was neither. Sheriff Terry poked his head in.

"How are you this morning?" he asked.

"None the worse for my experience," I answered, waving him in. "They've taken great care of me, but I have to tell you I'm ready to get out of here."

"Dixie was pulling into the parking lot when I crossed to the entrance," he said. "So, she should be here in a few minutes."

"I can't wait." I sighed.

"In the meantime, I wanted to ask you a few questions," he said.

"That's great timing, because I want to ask you some questions as well."

"Shall I go first?" he asked, getting out his notebook.

I nodded.

"Tell me, if you can, what you remember about the mailbox. Was there anything you noticed when you approached or before you opened it?"

"You mean, before it exploded?"

"Yeah, before it exploded."

"Nothing looked out of place. At least not that I remember. When I opened it, it seemed extremely full. I remember wondering if that was only one day's worth of mail." I paused, thinking.

Had there been anything else? No, a regular mailbox.

"And then I pulled out some of the mail and dropped a couple of envelopes. And boom, it exploded," I finished.

"Probably reaching down to get those letters you dropped kept you from being badly injured."

"Sometimes you get lucky." I took a breath. Truly, I did feel lucky. "Any clues on who planted the bomb?"

"A few, but nothing conclusive." He shook his head. "Because it involved mail, it's a federal offense and so now the feds will join in."

"That'll be good, right?" More people power.

"It actually will. They have access to some resources and tools that we don't have." He put his notebook away. "Now, your turn."

"When you came to Arbor House you were about to fill us all in on something. I assumed it had to do with Colette's death. What were you about to say?"

"I hadn't told the family about the note or the necklace that you found in the coin purse," he explained. "I'd wanted some idea what we were dealing with first. But I had some news."

I waited.

"We had been able to locate Libby, thanks to some credit card receipts. Her name is Elizabeth Black and Minnesota authorities have located her for us."

"How does that play out?" I asked. "Do you have to wait on some sort of official extradition?" I was impressed I'd remembered the word for it, but I wasn't sure how it actually worked. My knowledge of the process was a product of reading crime novels and watching the Mystery Channel.

An amused expression crossed his face. "We don't have anything to charge her with so right now she's just a person of interest."

Okay, so maybe I remembered the word, but wasn't up to speed on how it worked in real life.

"We've asked her to come in for questioning and she'll be talking to us tomorrow."

"But she can't be involved in this mail bomb. Not if she wasn't even in the state."

"Depends on the type of explosive." He shrugged. "You don't always have to be close by."

"Gosh, and she seemed like a nice enough person."

"Remember that's always what the neighbors say about serial killers." Terry raised a brow.

There was a light knock on the door and it eased open. Dixie had arrived and was carting my small travel suitcase. Terry jumped up to hold the door and help her with the luggage.

"I'm so glad to see you," I said, smiling at my friend. "But you do know I'm only going home, not on vacation?"

"I couldn't figure out what to bring for you to change into. It's kind of warm out there today." She blew bangs out of her eyes. "So I brought you a few options." She reached up and lifted auburn curls off her neck.

Sheriff Terry stood mesmerized.

"It's okay, I'm going in there to change." I pointed at the bathroom. "You two can stay and talk."

Neither answered me.

"Hello!" I snapped my fingers.

"What?" They both came to at once.

"I said, I'm going in the bathroom to change and I only have one request."

"What's that?" Dixie asked.

"I am going to ask you to cover your eyes until I get across the room, because I can't figure out how to keep this hospital gown closed in the back."

Dixie and Terry both obediently put their hands over their eyes. I grabbed the handle of the suitcase and started wheeling it toward the bathroom just as there was another tap on the door.

It was Nurse Jamie. She looked at Dixie and the sheriff with their hands still covering their eyes, and then looked at me. "I'm not even going to ask what's going on here."

I grinned at her. "I'm trying to get to the bathroom to get changed without flashing my friends."

"Your friends can wait in the hall." She pointed toward the door.

"Give me a few minutes," she told them as they went out. "I'll help Ms. Calloway get dressed. And then you all can continue with…whatever."

In short order she laid the suitcase on the bed, let me select what I wanted to wear, suggesting something easy to take on and off because she predicted I was going to be sore. With her assistance, I quickly changed into a pair of yoga pants and a soft V-neck knit top.

Then she ordered me to sit down and opened the door, motioning Dixie and Sheriff Terry back in. "I'll be right back with a wheelchair."

"I don't need a wheelchair," I protested. "I can walk."

"Not a discussion," Nurse Jamie responded. "It's required."

I suddenly remember what else I'd wanted to ask the sheriff about. I'd barely opened my mouth when his cell phone rang.

"Sheriff Griffin," he answered. "What?" He listened for a few minutes. "I'll be right there."

We all waited.

"There's been a shooting. Someone shot at Jezzie as she turned off the highway headed toward Arbor House."

"Is she okay?"

"No physical injuries, but pretty shook up. According to the officer on the scene, the bullet barely missed her. It went right through the windshield of her car."

"Oh, my stars." When majorly stressed, sometimes my mother comes right out of my mouth.

"I'm headed there now." He shoved his cell phone in his pocket and turned to go.

"We'll follow." I stood.

"No. You. Won't." The sheriff had been almost out the door, but he turned back and gave us the I-am-law-enforcement-and-you-are-not glare.

"No. You. Won't." Nurse Jamie was back with a wheelchair in time to hear Sheriff Terry's statement.

He held the door for her so she could roll the wheelchair over to me.

"You will take her straight home." She pointed at Dixie.

"And you will follow the instructions that we went over, and that I've written out for you." She handed me a paper. "Just in case you forget."

I shifted to the wheelchair, still unhappy about it, but if that's what it took to break me out of the hospital, so be it.

Dixie walked out with the sheriff, on her way to pull the car up front per Nurse Jamie's instructions.

The trip in the wheelchair was short, but I still felt silly. There was nothing wrong with my legs, for Pete's sake.

Dixie was already at the hospital entrance and I climbed into the passenger seat. The doctor had been clear: No driving today for me. If I didn't have any problems once I got home, I could drive tomorrow. But no long drives by myself or plane trips for a couple of weeks.

"I hope you don't mind that I brought your vehicle rather than mine." Dixie pulled out from the hospital lot and onto a street marked Kenyon Road.

"No problem." I buckled my seat belt and settled back.

"I thought my pickup might be harder for you to get in and I wasn't sure how sore you were going to be. You went flying."

"Is the B and B on the way back to St. Ignatius from where we are?" I asked.

"It is not and even if it were, you heard Nurse Jamie."

"And Sheriff Terry," I reminded her.

"Yeah, but I think I'm more scared of Nurse Jamie." She smiled and turned right. Which I thought was east.

"Do you want me to set…?" I tapped the GPS on the dash.

"No, I think I've got it."

* * * *

Dixie took the turn off the highway and onto the street that would take us to the heart of St. Ignatius. She'd done the whole trip and didn't even need Matilda's help. The show-off.

I have to confess that by the time Dixie pulled into my driveway, I was kind of ready for a nap. She helped by carrying the suitcase in and getting me settled in my chair.

Before she left, she carried pillows and a blanket from upstairs and left them on the couch.

"Just in case you decide you want a nap," she explained. "I'm going to go take care of some things, but you have my cell if you needed anything."

Ernest came to check me out and make sure I was okay. He might have really been checking to be sure I hadn't brought another dog home, but I liked to think he was concerned. He curled up on my lap.

Dixie had not been gone very long when I felt my eyes getting heavy. I didn't make it to the couch, but my chair was pretty comfortable.

I woke up with a start, hearing a knock on the door. Sitting up straight and disturbing my catnap partner, I started to get up to answer it when the door eased open. Ernest jumped down and went to investigate.

It was Max.

"Hello," he said quietly. "I'm sorry. You were asleep, weren't you?"

"Caught me." I smiled.

"Probably the best thing for you." He crouched down and looked me over. His sharp blue eyes searched my face. "Are you truly okay?"

"I am truly okay." I smiled.

He smiled back, his relief clear.

"Oh, I almost forgot. Dixie sent lunch for you." He handed me a bag. "I'm not sure what she sent, but if you need a plate or silverware, let me know."

"What I really need is water," I said. "Would you mind?"

"No problem." He went through to the kitchen and I could hear him opening cupboards.

"To the right of the sink," I called.

Max was back in a few minutes with a glass of water and a plate.

I opened the bag to find my favorite chicken club from the Red Hen Diner. Max had been smart to bring a couple of napkins.

Once he had my lunch arranged, he sat down in the chair across from me.

"Where's the d-o-g?" He spelled it out.

"Trying to stay out of trouble with Ernest?" I asked.

"You bet." He grinned.

"He spent the night with Greer," I answered. "When they decided to keep me at the hospital overnight, she offered. Dixie is going to pick Frenchie up later and drop her off."

I took a bite of the sandwich and leaned my head back. "This is so good. There's plenty if you're hungry."

"I already had lunch, but thank you."

There was another knock on the door and Max got up to answer it. This time it was Sheriff Griffin.

He followed Max to the living room, sank down on the couch, and leaned back against the cushions.

"What's up?" Max asked. "You look worse than Sugar."

I gave Max a look.

"Not that you look bad," he corrected quickly.

"He does look bad," I agreed. "But I think you could have worded that a little better."

"Now that we all concur that I look like hell…" Terry leaned forward, elbows on his knees. "How are you feeling?"

"Better than I did," I answered. "I slept most of the morning. Dixie sent lunch with Max. I'm being waited on hand and foot, so I'm feeling pretty good right now."

"Did she share the doctor's orders with you?" he asked Max.

"No, she didn't." He looked around. "But I'll bet I can find them."

"How is Jezzie?" I asked.

"Better than the Corvette." He shook his head.

"Wait, I thought that was Tom's car." He'd driven away in it that day when he and Jezzie argued.

"It is," Terry confirmed. "But for some reason Jezzie had borrowed it and that's what she was driving when she was shot at."

"I'll bet Tom was not happy about that." I shook my head. "I mean it's all bad, but bullet holes in the Corvette…"

"I've got to get going." Terry stood. "I wanted to check in and make sure you were doing okay. It sounds like Max and Dixie have you taken care of, but if you need something, give me a call."

"Thanks, Terry."

Max walked Terry to the door. I could hear them talking but couldn't quite hear what they were saying. When Max came back, he picked up my plate and carried it to the kitchen.

"Can I get you anything else?"

"No, to tell you the truth, I'm wiped out."

"You have my cell number; call if you need anything."

"You've already gone above and beyond, Max."

He gave me a careful kiss and reiterated the offer.

They were all acting like I was an invalid and while I appreciated their concern, I intended to get back to work tomorrow.

But first a nap.

Chapter Sixteen

The next morning, I arrived at the office early. Getting dressed had been a little difficult. Nurse Jamie had been right: I had more sore spots than I had that first day. I was glad Greer had offered to keep Frenchie another day because walking the frisky pooch would have been challenging.

I started the coffee and unlocked the front door.

As I waited for my morning cup of sanity to be ready, I sat down at my desk and booted up my computer before I remembered that I hadn't asked Dixie about all our materials from the Arbor family cookbook project. I didn't know if she'd remembered to get them or not in all the excitement the day of the mailbox bomb.

I got up and poured a cup. She should be in shortly and I'd ask her then.

I heard the bell over the door ding. I walked out front, expecting Disco in search of an afternoon snack, or Harry Harrison in search of signatures for his petition.

Instead it was Jezzie Arbor née Carr. It was hard for me to think of her as anything but Arbor because with all the siblings, and with her in particular, those family roots went deep. Or at least the company roots did.

As always, she looked like she'd just walked out of a board meeting. Apparently, none the worse for her close call.

"So, this is the center of the Sugar and Spice Cookbook operation?" she asked.

Was she being snarky? I searched her perfectly made-up face, but didn't see signs of an implied put-down, just interest.

"Yes, it is."

"Those are amazing photos. Done by your photographer friend?"

I nodded.

She crossed the room and walked up close to the oversized prints of Max's work that we'd hung on the largest of the walls. They were photos from our very first cookbook for the St. Ignatius Founders Day Celebration. Max had had them enlarged and framed. She was right—they were amazing.

Gallery-quality amazing. You weren't sure it you were looking at fine art or food, but in any case, you got hungry just looking at them.

I could tell she was picturing what Max could do with all the dishes from Arbor Foods, but I wouldn't give out Max's info without asking him first.

"But…" She sighed and walked back to where I stood by the counter, her heels clicking on the tile floor. "That's not why I'm here."

I waited.

"You and your partner have done an excellent job with our family cookbook project." She paused to reach inside her handbag. "But I'm afraid we can't go forward with it."

"We're nearly done with—" She cut me off.

"Here's a check." She held it out to me. "For all the work you've done."

"But—"

"With the death of that unfortunate girl…" Jezzie ran manicured fingers along the smooth surface of the counter.

I'm sure she meant the unfortunate death, not that Colette was unfortunate. But was the transposition a Freudian slip?

"And now the mailbox bomb, I've been shot at, and all of these death threats," she continued. "None of us can even think about anything but staying safe while we figure this out."

And sorting out the PR nightmare, I finished in my head.

I wondered if the sheriff was any closer to who might want to harm members of the Arbor family.

I looked down at the check. It was nearly double our cancellation fee. "Jezzie, I can't take this. It's too much."

"No, we discussed it." She extended it again. "And we feel this is right."

"But—"

"Sugar, you could have been badly injured by that mail bomb."

"But I wasn't." I put the check down on the counter.

Was that what this was about? Did they think that I might sue over the incident?

As much as I hated abandoning a project that we'd invested a lot of time in, one that was almost complete, and more importantly one that had such potential, it was clear they'd made up their minds. And the amount they'd offered in payment would allow me to pay Max, Liz, and others who had already provided services.

"I understand where you're coming from and I'm sure Dixie will too." I swallowed, feeling more attached to the project than I'd realized. "Promise me, once this is all sorted out, that if you think about resurrecting the cookbook idea, that you'll give us a chance again."

"You've got it." Jezzie reached out and shook my hand. A good, firm business grip. And then she took her exit.

I felt like I was crossed off her to-do list for the day.

I was still sitting at the counter when Dixie arrived. I could hear her putting things away and knew she'd stopped off at the store on her way.

"Hey," she called. "I see you made it okay."

"Hey," I answered.

"What's going on?" She came out from the back. "That didn't sound like a happy 'hey'."

"We've been fired." I handed her the check. "The Arbor family doesn't want to go forward with the cookbook."

She eyed the check and I could tell when she spotted the amount. "This is too much."

"That's what I said." I stood, needing to move around. "Jezzie said they'd talked about it and felt this was an appropriate amount."

"They're just hoping you don't file a lawsuit over that mailbox bomb."

"I wondered about that." I walked around the counter, peering at the lower shelves. Sometimes Dixie stashed baking experiments there. "But she didn't ask me to sign anything or even verbally promise anything."

"Still, I'll bet that's part of it."

"I agree," I said from where I crouched.

"What are you doing?" she asked.

"I'm trying to find where you've stashed the treats," I replied. "I'm hungry."

"They're right here." She opened one of the compartments and pulled out a plate of lemon bars.

"Wow, those look yummy." I plucked one off the plate and took a bite.

"You look like you're feeling better," she noted, taking a bar for herself. "You've got some color today."

"I do feel better, but I'm really disappointed about the cookbook." I took another bite. "And my step-tracker thinks I died. It keeps sending me messages, because it can't figure out how I went from ten thousand steps to fifty."

Dixie laughed. "There's plenty of time to get back to your walking."

"Well, I'm going to get some steps in this morning after I take care of a few things." I grabbed a paper towel and wiped off my fingers. "As soon as I answer a few emails, I'm going to the sheriff's office to sign my statement about the mailbox bomb."

"Do you want me to take you?" she asked. "I need to sign mine as well."

"Sure, if you need to go anyway, we could go together." I didn't want to confess, but I'd only been there once and I wasn't exactly sure how to get there. St. Ignatius was small, but I'd been known to lose my way a time or two.

"Okay, let me know when you're ready."

I made short work of the emails, closed out the Arbor family account, and made out a deposit for Jezzie's check, then I wandered into the kitchen where Dixie was taking a couple of loaves of banana bread out of the oven.

She sat them on hot pads to cool and looked up. "Are you ready?"

"I'm ready," I answered. "Are you vying with Hilda for the best banana bread?"

"No," she corrected. "I'm using Hilda's recipe. We'll see if it's as good."

"Let's get this over with." I went back to the office to collect my keys and handbag.

"Do you want to drive or just give me directions?" I asked.

"Why don't you let me drive?" She held her hand out for the keys. "It will be quicker."

"Not going to argue with that." I handed over the keys and climbed into the passenger seat.

It was a short trip to the sheriff's office though it was near the edge of town. We got out and Dixie pushed the remote to lock the Jeep.

It seemed like you shouldn't need to lock your car in the parking lot of the county sheriff's offices. It would be pretty dumb to break into a car with that much law enforcement around, but I suppose criminals aren't always smart.

The Jameson County Sheriff's Office was a newer brick building and I reached to open the heavy plate glass door. It opened way too easily because someone was on their way out.

The someone was Libby.

"You," she huffed when she spotted me.

I wasn't sure why she was so mad at me, unless the sheriff had shared the fact that it was me who had noticed the necklace she wore.

Dixie moved forward and put her arm protectively between Libby and me.

"I guess you've been to see the sheriff?" I asked.

She nodded, her expression still angry.

"You knew Colette, then?"

"Her name was Amy." She touched the necklace she wore and her face suddenly crumbled. "Her name was Amy and she was my sister."

"I am so sorry for your loss." I touched her arm.

She jerked her arm away. All at once, Angry Libby was back.

"Don't get me wrong. I hated her." She swiped at tears. "But I didn't kill her."

She pushed between us, headed across the parking lot.

Dixie and I looked at each other.

"Wow." I finally broke the silence. "I'm not sure which part of that is harder to wrap my brain around."

"Our mail bomb statements will be pretty anticlimactic after that, huh?" Dixie held open the door. "After you."

Sheriff Terry was tied up at the moment, the young deputy at the front desk told us. We offered to come back but he asked us to take a seat. In a few minutes, Terry came out with two deputies in tow. They would be working with us. We could write up our accounts of the mail bomb incident and sign them and then we were free to go.

"We ran into Libby on our way in," Dixie mentioned as she stood.

"Ah." I could see the realization in his eyes. "We'll talk about that later. Right now, if we could get the statements out of the way?"

"No problem." We followed the two deputies back through the offices and to their interview room area.

The older female deputy showed me to a room and the younger one escorted Dixie to a different room. I could see that it would be helpful to hear the accounts from each of us with our own memories of what happened.

It didn't take long and we got done about the same time, Dixie a few minutes before me. The two deputies walked us back through the offices and to the front. They must have let Sheriff Terry know we were finished because he showed up at the front desk.

"I'll walk out with you." He punched in a code to open the gate that separated the counter from the reception area.

It was a short walk to the Jeep and he didn't speak until we got to the car. "As you know, Libby Black came in today and we interviewed her about the woman you knew as Colette."

"But she was really Amy Black," I blurted out.

"Right." He shook his head. "Do you have my office bugged?"

"She spotted us going in," Dixie explained. "We talked to her."

"She said Amy was her sister and she hated her but didn't kill her," I added.

"Pretty much what she told us too." He let out a sigh.

"Do you believe her?" Dixie asked.

Terry wiped a hand over his face. "Funny thing is, I do."

"I do too." I couldn't say why, but I did. I also had a sense that while she said she hated her sister, there was more to it than that.

Terry didn't move to leave.

"Was there something more?" Dixie asked.

"Just before you got done with your statements, I got a call from J.J. at Arbor House."

"And?" I held my breath. What now?

"And, they had a break-in this morning, or sometime during the night. Both the downstairs study and the upstairs library had been ransacked. Completely trashed."

"How did the person get in?" Dixie asked.

"They're not sure. Maybe the back door wasn't locked. You'd think they'd be more careful." Terry scuffed at the ground. "But that's not the worst of it. Lucinda is missing."

"What?" I gasped. "Has she been kidnapped?"

"We don't know." He shook his head. "I've got a team up there right now. With the threats, we're concerned that…"

He didn't finish the thought, but we got it.

* * * *

The drive back to the office didn't take us long and we were both quiet, lost in thoughts of these new developments.

Their mailbox bombed. One of them shot at.

And now, a break-in. And Lucinda missing.

"I can only imagine how the sheriff is going to feel having to break that news about Colette's real identity to Theo and the rest of the Arbor family," Dixie said, as we went through the back at the Sugar and Spice offices. "I wonder how they'll react. All this has to be connected in some way."

"We'll never know," I said. "Because we're fired."

"Hard for you to let this one go, huh?"

"It is," I answered. "We don't usually spend this much time with our clients. Or get to know them this well."

"That's true." Dixie headed toward the kitchen.

"Remind me to not ask any of the backstory of the sorority sisters or the Mississippi River people on these next projects, okay?" I said as I dropped off my bag in the office and went to unlock the front door. "No personal stuff. Get the recipes. Make the cookbook."

"Right. Like that's going to happen," I heard from the other room.

When I got back to my desk there were a couple of slices of fresh banana bread on a saucer in the middle of my paperwork.

"You are the reason I have to walk so many miles every day." I said it loud enough I was sure Dixie could hear me.

"If you don't want it, just toss it," she called back.

"Like that's going to happen," I muttered as I took a bite.

* * * *

We worked for a couple of hours on our own. Me in the office and Dixie in the kitchen.

I heard a growl and realized it was my stomach. Glancing up at the clock, I realized we'd worked right through lunch, probably in part because of the banana bread. I picked up the saucer and looked at it. Nothing but crumbs there and only a few of those.

"How was it?" Dixie stood at the door of the office.

"Amazing," I answered. "But now I'm hungry and it's past lunchtime."

"Want me to bring you something?" she asked. "Or we can run over to the Red Hen?"

"I don't think I'm up to the interrogation just yet." I made a face. I knew word of the mail bomb had to have reached St. Ignatius and I'd been a little surprised we hadn't had visitors today. "If you're going to be stopping someplace where you can bring me something, that would be great."

"You've got it." She slung her purse over her shoulder. "Any preferences?"

"None." I was hungry. And not picky. "Surprise me."

"I won't be long." She went out the back.

Dixie hadn't been gone more than five minutes when I heard the bell ding out front.

I'd spoken too soon on our absence of visitors.

I set aside my paperwork and walked out front, expecting Disco or maybe even Lark from next door, but not expecting the mountain of a man who walked in.

He strode across the floor and held out a beefy hand. "Hello, I'm Glue Man."

Well, sure you are.

Several thoughts went through my head.

First off, he must have a real name. I mean, his driver's license surely doesn't say *First name: Glue. Last name: Man.* Right?

Secondly, I couldn't imagine he was the man they glued to the steel beam to demonstrate how strong the glue was. I still hadn't seen the ad, but they surely had to use some skinny guy. This guy, no way. His bright green T-shirt and crisp overalls gave new meaning to the big and tall sizes.

"Nice to meet you. I'm Sugar." I held out my hand and hoped he didn't hurt me.

"Why, it could not be lovelier to meet you." His handshake was firm but not crushing. I guess when you looked like him you had nothing to prove.

"I didn't know you'd moved in already." I'd thought nothing was happening until the first of next month.

"Oh, no," he boomed. "I haven't. I'm just here meeting people."

"I see." Though I wasn't sure I did.

"I understand there has been some trepidation about my business coming to town." He lowered his voice as if it were a secret.

I could assure him there was nothing secret about it. Harry Harrison had been very vocal about his concerns.

"I think the Square Merchants Association may have sent your company some questions about the operation," I said.

"That's right!" He answered so loud I jumped. We were back to full volume. "And I'm here to answer them."

"Hmm." I wanted to ask him to use his "inside voice" but I wasn't sure he had one.

"Tonight!" He slammed a card down on the counter and I feared for our fancy quartz surface. "Tonight, we are havin' a meeting at the chicken restaurant and I will answer everyone's questions."

He waved his hands in the air as if he'd be presenting an oracle where all life's questions would be answered.

I picked up the card, which simply said: Glue Man Group Meeting, Red Hen Diner, 7PM. That's what I'd thought he meant by "chicken restaurant" but it was good to have confirmation.

"I hope you can come." And with that, Glue Man gave a salute and lumbered out.

I was still standing in stunned silence when he popped back in. "I almost forgot. Here's a glue sample for you." He tossed a bright green tube on the counter. "Be careful with it. It works fast and it's strong!" He flexed his massive arms and gave a big grin. And then he was gone again.

I waited for a few minutes to be sure he wasn't coming back before I picked up the tube of glue to look at it.

That's where I was still standing when Dixie got back with our lunch.

"What's that?" she asked.

"Glue Man glue," I answered. "He was here."

"Glue Man was here?"

"Yep, and you missed it. He was huge." I held up my hands. "And loud."

"Well, come on back and pick which salad you want and let's have some lunch. You can tell me about it."

No hesitation on my part. Dixie had picked up salads from the deli at the grocery store and they looked fabulous. I grabbed the Cobb salad and we scooted stools up to the counter.

After discussing my Glue Man encounter and talking about the meeting planned for tonight, we decided we didn't both necessarily have to be there.

"Let me take this one," Dixie insisted. "I'll explain that you're still recovering."

"Man, I hate to throw you under the bus on this one, but just the thought of listening to Glue Man shout for an hour makes my head hurt."

"No worries." She waved a plastic fork at me. "I've got this one."

"Thanks, I appreciate it."

"But I am keeping track and you'll owe me big-time." She grinned.

"Remember, I have this glue." I waved the green tube at her. "And I'm not afraid to use it."

Chapter Seventeen

As it turned out, I needed that tube of glue sooner than I'd thought. When I walked in the front door at my house, it appeared either I'd had a break-in or my two furry roommates had had a party. Or a fight.

I was betting on the last one.

When I let myself in and stepped into the living room, two innocent faces looked up at me. Frenchie peered out from her carrier where she'd been snuggled against the soft blue knit: What was left of Colette's sweater.

"Amy's sweater," I corrected myself. I needed to start calling her by her real name.

I shifted my gaze to Ernest, who looked up from his place on the back of my easy chair. He blinked his eyes at me as if he'd been asleep since I'd left that morning.

"What have you two done?" I said sternly, looking from one to the other.

All the genealogy papers from Lucinda that I'd been looking through the night before were scattered across the floor. I pictured a cat-vs.-dog race atop the coffee table that had sent them flying.

Picking up the papers, I stuffed them back in the manila envelope. I'd put them in order later. It had been kind of Lucinda to share them with me. She'd been at this research a long time and she was right—it did help to see the types of public documents that were available. Cemetery listings, records of land sales, business transactions that had been filed, and even plats of towns that no longer existed.

I worried about what had happened to her. Sheriff Terry had said he'd let us know if there was any word, but they were still trying to piece together exactly what had actually transpired. How had someone gotten in? Why hadn't the others heard anything?

As I grabbed a couple of papers that had landed near the bookcase, I noticed a vase had also been knocked to the floor.

Unlike the one that had shattered the first night I'd arrived home with Frenchie, this vase was not an inexpensive yard sale find. It was a vintage Fostoria vase, a gift from my Aunt Celia. I really liked the light blue color. It was a clean break, so perhaps the Glue Man super-fixative would be able to repair it.

Placing the two pieces on the coffee table, I glared at the two culprits. "I should have known better than to leave you two home alone."

Frenchie gave a little whimper at my harsh tone and I immediately felt bad. Ernest looked at me and then twisted his head to look around the room, as if he couldn't figure out who I was talking to. I sighed.

I plucked the glue sample from my bag and laid it on the table with the vase pieces and then headed upstairs to change before tackling the job. Not wanting to chance dripping something that could glue a guy to a steel beam onto my good clothes, I changed into jeans and an old cotton top.

As I came back downstairs, I remembered I hadn't taken Frenchie out. I'd been so focused on cleaning up the mess that I'd forgotten. This dog-sitter thing took some attention.

I quickly clipped the leash onto her collar and we headed outside.

It was getting dark earlier and next door, Mrs. Pickett had her porch light on. There were bags of leaves on her curb.

I glanced with satisfaction at the bags of leaves on my curb as well.

See there, I can be a responsible homeowner.

I wanted to stick out my tongue in the direction of her house, but thought it might ruin my "responsible homeowner" status. Though I wasn't truly a homeowner yet, but Greer had begun talking about selling again. If she could just hang on a little longer, I'd soon be in a better place to buy the house.

Frenchie and I did a short walk up the street and back. Returning home, I realized I was hungry. It had been a while since those salads Dixie had picked up. I decided to eat a quick bite before tackling the aftermath of the Ernest and Frenchie chase scene.

Unlatching Frenchie's leash, I hung it on the coat hook by the door and headed to the kitchen to see what I could find to eat.

I heard the knock at my front door but wanted badly to ignore it.

What could Mrs. Pickett want now? Was my grass not growing straight? Had my leaves fallen on her side of the fence again? Or, heaven forbid, were my weeds jumping the fence?

Whatever it was, I was sure it wasn't good.

Scratching Ernest's head as I passed, I headed to the front door.

Opening it a crack, I was surprised it wasn't Mrs. Pickett. It was a tall man with a dark hoodie covering his head and most of his face.

"Can I come in?" a low voice asked.

"Uhm, no." I wasn't about to let some guy I didn't know in my house. I started to push the door closed.

"Sugar, it's me," a female voice choked out breathlessly. Her hand reached up and lifted the hood so I could see her face.

Good grief, it was Lucinda!

"Everyone is so worried about you." I grabbed her in a hug and pulled her inside. "What's going on?"

"Close the door quick." She pushed it shut. "I'm not sure that I haven't been followed."

"Come into the living room." I took her by the arm. She was shaking.

"I need—" Lucinda tried to catch her breath. "I need—"

"Take your time." I tried to keep my voice calm but I was worried about her. She looked like she might pass out. "Let's sit down."

"I can't." She twisted her hands and then reached out and grabbed my wrist. "Sugar, you won't believe this but I think—"

KNOCK! KNOCK! KNOCK!

We both jumped at the pounding on the door.

"Go on in there until I find out who it is." I motioned for Lucinda to move out of sight in the kitchen.

Had she been followed? It could be the person who was threatening the Arbor family members. I didn't want to take any chances.

I eased open the door and peered out.

Mrs. Pickett.

She wore her favorite pink chenille bathrobe; her hair was rolled in those pink foam rollers that went out of style several decades ago. A blue gingham dish towel tied the rollers tight to her head instead of a scarf. Yellow rain boots completed the ensemble.

"You can't use those trash bags."

"What trash bags?" The quickest way to deal with her was always to hear whatever her complaint was. Otherwise she wouldn't move on. Which I needed her to do. Now.

"Those." She pointed at the paper bags of leaves I'd raked a few days ago. I'd had Max help me place them on the curb for collection. "They won't take them."

"I got them at the grocery store and they told me they were the right ones."

"They were wrong." She pulled a bag out from under her bathrobe and held it out so I could see. "You gotta have this kind."

"Okay, thanks." I reached for it and she snatched it back, tucking it under her robe again. Well then, the bag had apparently just been for show-and-tell.

So off you go, then.

"Get them at Harrison's Hardware, not at the grocery store."

"Got it." I appreciated the advice even if the delivery left a lot to be desired. However, I had a missing person hiding in my kitchen and I needed Grumpy to move along.

She narrowed light blue eyes, watching me.

Did she expect me to rush to the hardware store right now?

"Thanks so much. I'll get them tomorrow." I stepped back and moved to close the door.

A booted foot stopped me.

"Those will blow around." She pointed at the wrongly bagged leaves. "You'll hafta put them in your garage till you get the right bags."

"I'll do that." Pushing the door closed, I heard her clomp across the porch and down the steps.

"Lucinda," I called. "Sorry about that. It was my next-door neighbor all in a fuss about me using the wrong leaf bags."

I stepped into the kitchen and looked around.

Lucinda was gone.

Chapter Eighteen

I walked through the kitchen and looked in the laundry room.

"Where did she go?" I asked Ernest and Frenchie, who had followed me.

I checked the hallway that led to the back of the house and the basement stairs with the two on my heels, though I think they were less interested in Lucinda and more interested in if I planned to feed them any time soon.

"Lucinda?" I called again.

Where on earth had the woman gone? I couldn't imagine that she'd slipped past me and headed upstairs, but I'd check anyway.

Halfway up the stairs, I called her name again. "Lucinda?"

There was a loud knock on the door. Had she gone out the back for some reason when I was talking to Mrs. Pickett and now come around to the front? I hurried down the stairs.

"Luc—" I pulled open the door, but it wasn't Lucinda. This time it was Jezzie.

Good grief, that was fast. Had Lucinda called her to come and pick her up? I had no idea how Lucinda had gotten to my place and I also didn't know how I was going to explain having lost her in such a short time.

"Hello, Sugar," Jezzie said, stepping inside. As usual she was dressed to the nines: A navy skirt, a soft blush blouse, and matching four-inch heels.

I felt like a slouch in my jeans and a top that had seen better days. Still, I hadn't been expecting company. Frenchie went back to her carrier and Ernest jumped on the arm of the sofa, watching this new visitor but keeping an eye on Frenchie.

"Please come in," I replied, although she'd already moved into the entryway.

"I'll get right to the point." She straightened the pearls at her neck. "I understand Lucinda gave you some papers the other day."

"She did." I nodded slowly as it dawned on me that Lucinda had not called her. Interesting timing. I immediately went on high alert. "Some things to help me with my research on my father's biological parents."

I motioned for her to have a seat.

"I'll need those papers." She continued to stand.

Well, that was kind of rude.

"What possible interest do you have in my family?" I stalled, trying to make sense of the demand.

"Just get them," she bit out.

"I don't think so." I frowned at her.

The Arbor family had been through a lot, between the murder of an almost-family member and the threats against other family members, but there was no excuse for barging into my home and barking orders.

"Get them for me."

That's when I noticed the handgun she'd pulled from her purse.

Suddenly the missing piece of the puzzle slid into place. I stepped backward into the living room. I didn't know what the heck was in those papers, but I knew I would hand them over rather than get shot.

"They're right over there." I pointed toward the table.

She motioned with the gun. "Get them."

Well, there went my rather naive thought that I'd just hand them over. That my cooperation would prevent me being shot. That she'd take them and leave. I eased toward the table and reached for the envelope where I'd stuffed all the papers.

The determination on Jezzie's face told me she wasn't going to simply accept the envelope and go. I didn't know how she'd explain away my death, but I was sure she had some plan.

Could I buy some time?

"So, it's been you all along," I said.

She nodded, a bit of a proud smirk on her face.

"But you killed the wrong person." I'd figured out Colette aka Amy hadn't been the target, but I hadn't known who had been.

A shadow passed over her face. "That stupid girl grabbed Lucinda's coat to take her dog out."

"And then instead of a potential hunting-accident scenario you had a full-scale police investigation on your hands and had to wait to try again."

She nodded, her perfectly coiffed hair not moving, her gun hand steady.

"I don't think the mailbox bomb would've killed her, though."

"Wasn't the intent." She smiled.

"Ah, you were trying to get rid of the DNA tests."

"Those ridiculous DNA tests were just a bonus. The idiot had already found out too much with all of her digging. If she was able to get everyone interested in digging up the past, there would be no stopping her."

"You were trying to kill her, then?"

"If I'd been trying to kill her, she'd be dead." Her dark eyes were cold. "I just wanted to send her to the ER, get her out of the house, so I could find her papers and get rid of them."

"Which you did when you staged the break-in."

"I destroyed everything and then she let it slip that she'd given you copies of some of the records." She stepped toward me. "Now give me those copies."

I'd held out hope that Lucinda was in hiding and was maybe waiting to surprise Jezzie. And save me. But I didn't see any evidence that she was still in the house.

I glanced down the hallway.

Could I make a run for it?

I didn't know if Jezzie was a crack shot in addition to being a champion archer, but she handled the gun like she knew what she was doing. Which meant my chances were not good.

Still, I'd been held at gunpoint before. I was not about to get shot without putting up a fight.

And I wasn't going to just hand over the papers she wanted and let her shoot me.

I leaned over the table, picked up the envelope and the Glue Man tube, squeezing a good glob of the glue onto the paper.

"Here you go." I held out the envelope, deliberately extending it toward her gun hand.

She shifted the firearm to her left hand and grabbed the papers from me. "They had better all be in here."

"Oh, everything is there," I assured her.

"What's this?" Jezzie suddenly registered the sticky substance on the papers I'd handed her. She tried to pull it loose but it stuck.

True to Glue Man's word, the stuff worked fast and it was strong.

Jezzie shook her hand to let go of the paper. She tried to put the gun back in her right hand but couldn't do it with the envelope stuck to her hand. In a hokey-pokey sort of move she shook her hand all around, trying to lose the envelope.

It would have been funny if it weren't so terrifying.

I ran for the stairs, thinking the bathroom door was the only door in the house that locked. I'd call 911 from the bathroom.

It was then I remembered my phone was in the kitchen.

I started back down, then quickly changed my mind. Even if she hunted me down, that would take her some time and maybe by that time I could come up with plan B.

Or if Jezzie fired the gun, Mrs. Pickett would likely call the police to report a violation of the noise ordinance at my house.

My legs felt like lead and I was babbling.

The babbling was all in my head, but still.

Get a grip, Sugar! I said in my best Aunt Cricket voice. In my head.

As I reversed course and headed back upstairs, Jezzie was right behind me, the gun clutched awkwardly in her left hand. She still flailed about with her right hand trying to get the envelope to let loose.

She grasped at me but couldn't get a hold. At the top of the stairs I stopped, took a big breath, and planted my feet.

Just as I was about to make my move, the front door burst open. It was Sheriff Terry with his weapon drawn. Jezzie turned her gun on him.

That's when I gave her a solid push that sent her down the stairs.

She teetered for a few minutes on those fancy four-inch heels and then down she went. When she reached the bottom, the sheriff kicked the handgun that had fallen with her out of her reach and grabbed her arms, holding her down face-first.

Thank you, Sheriff Terry. And thank you, Glue Man.

My knees gave out. I sat down on the stairs and dropped my head in my hands.

Chapter Nineteen

I don't know how long I sat on the stairs, but at some point Lucinda joined me. While I'd been chatting with Mrs. Pickett about leaf bags, she had spotted Jezzie's car. She had already put together some of the pieces and suspected Jezzie. Not knowing what else to do, she had knocked on Mrs. Pickett's door and asked to use her phone to call the sheriff.

I was never going to hear the end of that.

My driveway was packed with Jameson County Sheriff's Department cars. I wished they'd turn off their flashing lights. It wasn't just Mrs. Pickett—the flashing lights had also attracted the attention of most of the neighborhood. Which meant everyone was outside standing on their lawns, trying to figure out what was going on.

Sheriff Terry must have called both Dixie and Max because they arrived within minutes of each other.

The stairs were getting kind of crowded. I suggested we move to the living room. Frenchie was huddled in her carrier curled up in the blue knit, the excitement too much for her. I looked around for Ernest and found him under the couch. He eased out and came to make sure I was okay.

"Was there information in the papers you'd given me?" I eased down on the couch, still a little wobbly. "Jezzie was convinced there was, but was there really?"

"Actually, there was." Lucinda dropped into a chair and pushed up the sleeves of her sweatshirt. "I'd found a promissory note that gave my father one half of the company if the sum of five thousand dollars was not paid back. There was a copy in your packet."

"What?" I was shocked. She'd said the two family histories seemed to be entwined, but this was mind-boggling.

"I'd asked Marta about it and she knew Joe, Sr. had borrowed money to expand but didn't know from whom," she explained. "My father died suddenly when I was young and apparently he kept lousy records because none of this came to light."

"Did Jezzie know?" Max sat beside me on the couch, pushing a couple of the loose pillows behind my back.

Lucinda hadn't, to my knowledge, shared any of her discoveries with the rest of the family.

"She did know." Lucinda nodded. "Her father had told her and so she knew if I kept digging, there was a good chance I would eventually find enough to, if nothing else, begin to ask questions."

"That's when she decided to kill you and hoped it could be passed off as a hunting accident." Dixie walked in from the kitchen and handed me a freshly made cup of coffee.

"You're the best." I smiled up at her.

"Anyone else?" Dixie asked. "Sugar has not a lick of food in there, so I can't offer you anything to eat. But she has a whole cupboard full of different varieties of coffee and tea. And some gourmet hot chocolate."

It was the truth.

"I'll take a coffee." Sheriff Terry had joined us.

Dixie looked at the rest of the crew.

Max shook his head.

"Tea, if you don't mind," Lucinda answered. "Any type. Something strong would be great."

"You've got it." Dixie exited again.

"I let your husband know that you're okay and he's on his way to get you," Sheriff Terry said to Lucinda. "The rest of the story, I saved for when he gets here."

She nodded and leaned back in the chair, closing her eyes.

I couldn't even imagine that conversation.

Hello, dear. The good news is I'm found and I'm fine. The bad news is your sister tried to kill me.

Talk about a dysfunctional family. It certainly took the fun out of dysfunctional.

Dixie was back with coffee for Terry, who I was afraid had a long night ahead. And tea for Lucinda, who was handling it all amazingly well.

I was doing better. I had begun to get my bearings. I leaned forward and placed my half-empty coffee cup on the table and realized as I did that my other hand was cradled in Max's.

The simple gesture was comforting in a way that said far more than words could have.

Chapter Twenty

Dixie and I had delivered the final copies of the Arbor family cookbook to the family at Arbor House that afternoon. After all that had happened, being there again was both a bit disconcerting and strangely comforting. It was like everything had come full circle. A lot of questions had been answered. The cookbook project was complete and we'd brought enough copies for everyone.

With Jezzie's arrest the family had made the decision to leave the group photo out of the book. Instead we included several candid shots Max had taken during his visit.

Theo hadn't been present when we dropped off the cookbooks. He'd decided to get back to his life in Chicago and Gwen told us he'd agreed to work with a grief counselor. Not surprisingly, Tom also was missing. It turned out he had filed for divorce from Jezzie prior to the original family get-together and had agreed to attend only because she didn't want the rest of the family to know.

The rest of the family was picking up the pieces and holding on to each other. J.J. and Lucinda, Jonathan and Gwen, Marta, and in the strangest development of all, Hilda.

Jezzie had been concentrating on Lucinda and the information she had found showing an outstanding promissory note against the company, perhaps changing the balance of power. But there had been another wrinkle in her plans to expand.

Unbeknown to the others in the family, Jonathan and Gwen had done a DNA test a couple of years earlier and so his DNA was in the database. Hilda had recently done a test at the urging of her daughter and it had shown a match.

With Jonathan Arbor. A strong match.

Hilda wasn't just an Arbor relative; she was a half-sibling.

Many years ago, Joe, Sr. had an affair with Hilda's mother. But, as Hilda had told me, her mother died when she was very young, and her father shortly thereafter. And she was adopted by the Gentry family.

Marta had known about the affair and had suspected there was a child who she figured would one day contact the family. She hadn't realized that child was right under their noses.

I wasn't sure what that meant in terms of sharing the family fortune, but I'd bet it meant Hilda could get those corns fixed.

* * * *

After we had delivered the cookbooks, I dropped Dixie back at the office to pick up her car. I had one more thing to take care of.

I had contacted Libby, Colette's—or rather Amy's—sister, about Frenchie. She lived in an apartment that didn't allow pets and had no interest in the dog. She had asked if I could help with re-homing the pup and I'd found the perfect solution.

I stopped at home and gathered up Frenchie's toys. Tucking her into the carrier with the remaining ragged section of blue sweater, I patted her head.

"You can come back for a visit anytime," I promised.

She gave a small woof of approval.

Ernest meowed from the stairs.

"She can." I pointed a finger at him. "And you will be a welcoming host."

His tail swish said he understood, but didn't necessarily agree.

Carrying the small pink kennel to my car, I strapped her in and turned the Jeep toward the Good Life retirement complex.

Greer and Frenchie were perfect for each other.

"You two will be family," I told her.

Families. In the words of the philosopher, Hilda, "Sometimes you're born to them, sometimes you create them."

Recipes

The Arbor Family's Famous Quiche Lorraine

Crust

1 cup all-purpose flour
1/4 teaspoon salt
1/3 cup cold butter, cut into chunks
3–4 tablespoons cold water

Filling

8 slices crisply cooked bacon, crumbled
1/3 cup chopped onion
4 ounces (1 cup) shredded Swiss cheese
2 cups half-and-half
4 eggs
1/4 teaspoon salt
1/8 teaspoon pepper
1/8 teaspoon ground nutmeg
Dash of hot pepper sauce, if desired

Preparation

1. Heat oven to 375°F.

2. Combine flour and 1/4 teaspoon salt in bowl; cut in butter with pastry blender or fork until mixture resembles coarse crumbs. Stir in enough water with fork; just until flour is moistened. Shape dough into a ball; flatten slightly.

3. Roll out dough on lightly floured surface into 12-inch circle. Fold into quarters. Carefully place pastry into ungreased 9-inch glass pie pan. Carefully unfold pastry, pressing firmly against bottom and sides of pie pan. Trim crust to 1/2 inch from edge of pan. Crimp or flute edge.

4. Sprinkle bacon onto crust; top with onion and cheese. Combine all remaining filling ingredients in bowl; beat with whisk until well mixed. Pour over cheese in pan.

5. Bake 40–45 minutes or until center is set. Let stand 10 minutes before cutting.

Hilda's No-Fail Banana Bread

Ingredients

1 stick butter
3 large ripe bananas
2 large eggs
1 teaspoon vanilla extract
2 cups all-purpose flour
1 cup granulated sugar
1 teaspoon baking soda
1/2 teaspoon salt
1/2 teaspoon cinnamon

Preparation

Preheat oven to 350 degrees. Spray a loaf pan with nonstick cooking spray or grease with butter and set aside.

Add the stick of butter to a large bowl and microwave for 1 minute, or until melted.

Add the bananas to the same bowl and mash with a fork.

Add the vanilla extract and egg to the bowl and use the same fork to mash and stir until no yellow streaks of egg remain.

In a second large bowl whisk together the flour, sugar, baking soda, salt, and cinnamon.

Add the dry ingredients to the wet ingredients and mix together with a spatula just until combined.

Pour the batter into prepared loaf pan and bake for 45–55 minutes until a toothpick inserted in the center of the bread comes out clean.

Greer Gooder's Chicken Salad

Ingredients

2 large boneless, skinless chicken breasts cooked, chilled for a bit, and diced.
1 cup chopped celery
1 1/2 cups halved seedless red grapes
2–3 green onions, chopped
1 cup mayonnaise
1/2 cup sour cream
1 tablespoon lemon juice
1 teaspoon prepared yellow mustard
2 tablespoons chopped fresh parsley
1/2 teaspoon dried dill weed
1/2 teaspoon onion powder
1/2 teaspoon garlic powder
1 teaspoon sugar
1/2 teaspoon salt
1/2 teaspoon freshly ground black pepper
1/4 cup sliced almonds

Preparation

1. Place the diced chicken, celery, green onions and grapes in a large mixing bowl and stir to combine.
2. In a separate bowl, stir together the remaining ingredients (except for the almonds) until well mixed. Pour the mixture over the chicken salad and stir, making sure the chicken is thoroughly coated.
3. Cover and chill for at least two hours.
4. Sprinkle a few almonds on the chicken salad just before serving.
5. Greer serves her chicken salad on croissants, but you can use sandwich bread or wraps just as easily. Or if you've watching your carbs, it's also good on a bed of butter lettuce.

Acknowledgments

A book is always a project of the heart and this series, set in my home state, has allowed me to explore some places and emotions I hadn't visited in a long time. As Sugar learns in the story, sometimes you find family in unusual places.

A huge thank-you to my sisters of the heart and critique group: Tami, Cindy, Chris, and Anita. You are the best!

Love and bushels of thanks to my family for your love and understanding.

As always, to my editor John Scognamiglio and the dedicated crew at Kensington—thank you for your awesomeness. Your talents and expertise always make my story and my vision a much better book.

Super-agent Christine Witthohn, your belief in me keeps me going. You rock.

And last but never least, dear readers, you are the reason any of us storytellers write books.

Thank you for your notes and emails that tell me Sugar, Dixie, and all the St. Ignatius residents come alive for you. I love that you love them and I love to hear from you!

You can reach me through my website at: MaryLeeAshford.com

And if you sign up for my newsletter, you'll always be up-to-date on the latest news!

CPSIA information can be obtained
at www.ICGtesting.com
Printed in the USA
LVHW111136070720
659897LV00017B/756

9 781516 105090